Look for More Titles by Cassandra Chandler

WHISPERING HEARTS
LINGERING TOUCH

Other Works
CRAFTING A WRITER'S LIFE: Building a Foundation

Coming Soon

The Blades of Janus
PERIHELION

Nothing to Declare

The Department of Homeworld
Security
Book Thirteen

Cassandra Chandler

Copyright Page

This book is pure fiction. All characters, places, names, and events are products of the author's imagination or used solely in a fictitious manner. Any resemblance to any people, places, things, or events that have ever existed or will ever exist is entirely coincidental.

Nothing to Declare
The Department of Homeworld Security, Book Thirteen
Copyright © 2020 by Cassandra Chandler
Print ISBN: 978-1-945702-48-8
Digital ISBN: 978-1-945702-47-1
Edited by Eliza Sinclair

First eBook edition: June 2020
First print edition: June 2020
10 9 8 7 6 5 4 3 2 1

cassandra-chandler.com
P.O. Box 91
Mission, Kansas 66201

Dedication

For Eliza Sinclair—my fellow adventurer.

Don't miss out on any of the alien action.
Subscribe to Cassandra Chandler's newsletter at
cassandra-chandler.com!

Chapter One

"There is something wrong with me."

Sabrina shook her head as she steered around the last corner before the "Look Again Pet Parlor" building. How had she managed to get through her entire evening without realizing she'd left her phone at work?

She wasn't sure which was worse—that she hadn't noticed her phone was gone or that she felt compelled to retrieve it before finally getting some sleep. Her body made its opinion clear as she let out a long yawn.

She could have waited till morning to get her phone, but that would mean she couldn't be reached quickly in case of an emergency. People were counting on her to keep their pets safe and happy.

Harbor wasn't a big town, but she and her best friend, Kimmy, had worked hard to make a name for themselves in the surrounding counties. They were the best groomer and boarding facility for hundreds of miles. Miles that were mostly farmland dotted with other tiny towns, but still…

With the Winter Fair only a few days behind them, Sabrina's fingers were still stiff from plaiting the manes of a dozen horses in intricate designs with festive garlands woven in.

That was Kimmy's brilliant idea to drum up business. Show off how pretty they could make people's animals and raise enough money to expand their building. Then they could have individual pet rooms for the animals to stay in instead of their current kennels. Sabrina was all for that.

And the thing was, it had worked. There had been a huge influx of customers since the fair ended. Kimmy was thriving on it. Sabrina was starting to drag.

If it would help them provide a better home-away-from-home for the animals, she'd get through it, though. And at least she'd be able to jump right into bed when she got home. She was already in her pajamas under her coat—the thick fleece matching set covered in rainbows and unicorns.

She turned off her headlights before pulling into the farthest spot from the door, not wanting to disturb the current boarders any more than was necessary. It was bad enough they'd be hearing her car engine.

Maybe she'd just sleep in the office tonight. Again. There was a cot set up for her and everything. It was uncomfortable as heck, but she usually felt better staying near the pets she was caring for.

They only had two dogs with them at the moment, but they also had seven cats. Mrs. Simpkins had brought in her entire menagerie—named after the seven dwarves—while her house was being fumigated.

Sabrina tucked a few stray blond strands under her bright purple stocking cap as she stepped into the brisk air. The Winter had been comparatively mild, but it was still cold as heck this late at night.

She closed her car door as quietly as she could, then used her key to slip in the back door of the building. Her keys clinked loudly as she dropped them into her purse and she froze, eyes closed as she waited for the barking to start.

Nobody made a sound.

She shut the door, slowly moving deeper into the building. A shiver ran down her spine that had nothing to do with the chill air that had followed her inside. It took her overtaxed brain a moment to realize what was wrong— aside from the eerie silence.

There was a light moving around in the kennel room. She could see it through the frosted glass window on the door.

Sabrina had locked up after a final check on the animals. No one else should be there.

Kimmy might have come back to do some late night paperwork. Or maybe she'd forgotten her phone, too. But she would have turned on the lights to see better.

No. Someone had broken in and was... Doing what? Robbing the dogs? Stealing the cat toys?

Sabrina needed to call Sheriff Mariana. But the shop didn't have a landline, and her phone was probably in the room with whoever that was. She always spent the last part of her shift with their guests to make sure they were settled for the night.

What would anybody want with a tiny pet parlor in a town so small she could walk from one end to the other in twenty minutes? It didn't make sense for it to be a thief. But then, who else could it be?

It was probably some kind of prank from the local high schoolers. There was nothing else to do in Harbor.

Sabrina crept closer to the door, determined to surprise the kids and give them hell for whatever hijinks they were up to.

"You're sure this won't hurt them?" a man said.

Sabrina would have enjoyed the low timbre and richness of his voice if his words hadn't sent another chill down her spine.

"Of course it will not." The second voice was higher pitched and had a strange sibilance to it. "Now stop distracting me and let us continue our work."

Not high schoolers…

Sabrina's heartbeat picked up. Someone really had broken in. And they were doing something that might hurt the animals.

Was that why she hadn't heard any barking? Had they already done something to the dogs?

Rage overwhelmed her fear. She stuck her hand in her purse and pulled out her stun-gun, suddenly glad she'd given in to her grandpa's insistence that she always carry one, even in the small, "safe" town. Before she could talk herself out of it, she opened the door to the kennels, flicking the light switch on as she burst into the room.

"Don't move," she shouted, blinking against the sudden brightness.

The man inside was having a similar issue with the light. He held one hand high, shielding his eyes.

As he lowered his arm, he said, "I thought you were running active scans so we wouldn't be surprised."

Sabrina looked all around the room. Pancakes and Fluffy were sitting up in their kennels, mouths open in broad smiles and tails wagging as they looked at her from under the carefully styled white fur that dangled from their foreheads.

Not a hair on their furry little bodies seemed to be out of place. They even still had their bows on.

The cat kennels seemed as full as they'd been when Sabrina left. It was hard to count all the occupants while she was trying to keep watch on the intruder and…

Where was his accomplice? Sabrina had heard two distinct voices, but only saw the one guy.

The one super-hot guy.

He had short, light-brown hair and dark blue eyes with crinkles at the edges, as if he laughed a lot. His jaw was cut, his features strong—as well as his physique. She could see a lot of it, since he was just wearing a gray T-shirt that had a green design around the collar, and khakis, with what looked like boat shoes.

Doesn't this guy know it's Winter?

Movement on his broad shoulders brought her attention back up from his seasonally inappropriate outfit. She almost screamed as what she'd thought was a colorful design on his shirt collar lifted its head and flicked its long tail.

He had an iguana on his shoulders.

The biggest iguana she had ever seen. It had to be at least three feet long without counting its tail.

What the heck kind of burglar brought his pet lizard along with him when he broke into a grooming and boarding shop?

"We can explain," the guy said.

Another chill shivered down her spine at the reminder that he wasn't alone—and she wasn't thinking about the iguana. Sabrina quickly shifted to have her back to the wall. She kept one eye on the door so no one could sneak up on her.

"Where's your accomplice?" Sabrina demanded.

"Accomplice? I don't know what you mean."

"You were talking to someone a minute ago. Where are they?"

He looked over at the iguana. The exhaustion must really be taking its toll, because Sabrina almost thought the iguana looked back at him. Like a meaningful exchange was taking place.

"Look, this is all a misunderstanding," he said. "My name is Len and this is Cyan."

He gestured to the lizard as he took a step forward, but froze when Sabrina lifted her stun-gun higher. His gaze locked on it as if he hadn't noticed it before.

"Wait... Is that a projectile weapon?" His voice had risen and his eyes were wide.

"Projectile? You mean like bullets?" She shook her head. "It's a stun-gun."

Stop reassuring the bad guy, Sabrina!

Dang it, she really had to watch that. She quickly added, "It'll electrocute you if I shoot you with it, so don't try anything."

"Electrocute me?" His eyebrows rose. "That's insane."

"Insane? You're the one who broke into my shop and brought along your pet lizard."

The iguana narrowed its eyes and let out a loud hiss. Sabrina instinctively pointed her stun-gun at it, then realized Len was the bigger threat and brought it back to her first target.

"First of all, Cyan is not my pet," he said. "She's my friend."

Sabrina shook her head. This guy was sounding crazier by the moment.

"That does nothing to explain what you're doing here in the middle of the night messing with my boarders," Sabrina said.

"Boarders?"

The iguana let out a series of hisses, pops, and clicks. Sabrina didn't know they were so vocal. Len nodded and then shrugged.

"Oh, the animals," he said. "Why do they call them 'boarders', though?"

Sabrina blinked a few times as she tried to come up with an explanation for how he was interacting with his pet. The only one that seem feasible was also completely ridiculous.

He was talking to the iguana. And pretending—or imagining—that the iguana was talking back.

"I'm calling the police," Sabrina said.

Except she still didn't have her phone. She didn't see it anywhere.

Even more disconcerting, she still didn't see the woman he'd been talking to earlier. Unless he'd been talking to himself and just making up the other voice.

That was too creepy to think about.

Maybe the voice had come from the iguana.

She barely kept herself from laughing at the thought.

No more overtime. The first thing she was doing after getting out of this encounter was calling Kimmy and insisting on taking a few days off.

"There's no need to call the police," Len said. "We'll leave."

"Not until you explain what you're doing here in the first place."

He let out a huge sigh. "We're aliens."

Sabrina did laugh that time. The sound almost drowned out the litany of hisses, clicks, and grumbles from the lizard.

"Only in Harbor," Sabrina said. "Okay, look, *tourist*. You need to do better research. Harbor doesn't have the most alien encounters or even alien sightings. It has the most crackpots who tell stories about them."

Her face heated at too many memories to process. She berated herself for using the word "crackpot".

Not. Cool. Sabrina.

"Nothing has ever been verified," she went on. "For those of us who live here, it's a town joke. And you're sure as hell playing to the wrong audience with me."

"Crackpots?" He cocked his head to the side.

Of course, he would zero in on that word. Sabrina felt her face heat even more, her skin prickling and her arms twitching with the urge to hit something.

On cue, the lizard hissed and clicked, as if she was explaining it to him. How had he trained it so well?

"That's not a very nice word," Len said.

Something zinged in her chest—in a not-unpleasant way. She deepened her scowl to fight it off.

"The guy who broke into my shop and was talking about hurting my cats does not get to critique my choice of words," she said.

"We aren't going to hurt anyone. We just need some

DNA samples."

"DNA samples."

"Yes." He took a step forward, but again stopped when she raised the stun-gun higher. "A litter of kittens was recently born aboard one of our spaceships. They're exhibiting behavior that the Earthlings among us find unusual."

"The Earthlings. Right." Crazy as he was, the guy could spin a good story. "What kind of 'unusual behavior' are they exhibiting? Walking around on their back legs wearing a hat and a pair of boots?"

"Um, no. As limited as our experience is with this kind of life form, even we would have realized that was outside the norm. These cats are smart. Incredibly smart. They may have even sabotaged parts of the ship."

"Why would they do that?"

"To get the Chief Engineer's attention." He shrugged at her quizzical look. "Patches has a soft spot for her."

"Patches," Sabrina said. "And she's one of the super-intelligent space cats."

"Exactly. We need DNA samples from cats born on Earth—preferably a variety of them—to compare and use as a control group to see if there's been some sort of mutation with the cats on our ship."

"This is insane." She shook her head, trying to not get swept up in his story…with limited success. "Why come here?"

"Craig told us about the town, and when we learned about Marvin—"

All the rage from earlier when she'd thought he was threatening the cats crashed back into her, bringing along a slew of its friends.

Indignation. Frustration. And above all else, love.

Nobody messed with her family.

Sabrina pressed the trigger without consciously thinking about it. The darts flew out from the gun, striking the guy in the chest.

"Don't you dare bring my grandpa into this," Sabrina said.

Very consciously, she held down the button to deliver the charge.

Chapter Two

Len pinched his eyes shut, waiting for the current to flood his body. The Earthling—Sabrina—had said it was supposed to electrocute him. But nothing happened.

He opened one eye at a time, looking down at the needles embedded in his chest, then along the wires that still connected them to the weapon Sabrina was trying to use on him.

She seemed about as confused as he was. She angled the weapon to get a better view while inspecting it, then pointed it at him again and started pulling some sort of trigger over and over.

"Why won't this thing work?" she said.

Len reached up and grabbed the needles, carefully removing them from his chest. He dropped them to the ground, then pulled at the collar of his shirt so he could see the marks on his skin.

"You shot me with needles?" he said. "What kind of weapon is that? I thought you said it was going to electrocute me."

"It was supposed to!"

Cyan decided to interject, her translator deactivated so they could communicate semi-privately in the Vegan language that he'd recently had downloaded into his brain specifically for this mission.

"I have disabled her weapon," Cyan said.

Len let out a relieved breath. He responded in Sabrina's language. "We've disabled your weapon temporarily. Now we can have a civilized discussion."

"About 'Craig'?" Sabrina said.

The Earthling's face had turned bright red again. It was quite a contrast from the paleness of earlier. Her blue eyes practically sparked as she looked around the room. She picked up a canister filled with large grains of…sand or something, and hefted it with her free hand as if she was going to throw it at him.

"Wait a minute," Len said, backing away. "Put that down."

She grimaced, her gaze resting on Cyan for a moment.

"Crud," Sabrina said. "If I didn't think I might hit that iguana, I would totally bean you with this."

"Bean me?"

Cyan spoke again. "It is a colloquial expression that means she would throw the object at you, striking you soundly."

"Thanks, Cyan," Len said. "But it would be even more helpful if you'd back me up in English."

The Earthling was edging toward the door. Len quickly

moved closer to it, careful not to actually block her path. He didn't want to scare her—any more than she obviously already was. But he was concerned she'd reach out to the authorities she'd mentioned earlier. That could... complicate things.

"Please hear us out," he said. "I promise we won't hurt you."

"You and your 'alien iguana' friend." Sabrina set down the large tub of sand. "So reassuring."

"Your name is Sabrina Davis," Len said. "Your grandfather is Marvin Davis."

She opened her mouth to speak, a moment of confusion passing over her features, but then they settled back into the anger he was beginning to recognize.

"I told you to leave my grandpa out of this."

"But he's the reason we're here," Len said. "Craig reached out to him and Marvin let us know you were keeping several cats here that aren't related, giving us the perfect opportunity to collect a wide sample of—"

"There's no such thing as aliens!" Sabrina nearly shrieked. "I've had to listen to this my whole life from the townies, and I sure as heck am not going to put up with it from some stranger who's probably only out to write another satire piece about the crazies in Harbor who think that Bigfoot is a four-armed, blue-faced, white-furred space Sasquatch."

"Lyrian." Len spoke as gently as he could.

"What?" Sabrina bit out.

"Not space Sasquatch. Craig is a Lyrian."

She hissed in a breath through clenched teeth. "I hate you so much right now."

"You don't know me well enough to hate me." He smiled at her, but she only scowled harder.

"Really?" She arched an eyebrow at him and crossed her arms over her chest awkwardly, still holding onto that strange, ineffective weapon.

"Okay, this situation is… We got off to a bad start," Len said. "Can we just start over?"

"No."

Cyan let out a little hissing laugh.

Len looked over at the Vegan and said, "Not helping."

Cyan leapt off his shoulder, easily grabbing the metal of the nearest cage and clambering on top of it.

If he didn't know any better, watching her movements, he might be fooled into thinking she was just an ordinary lizard. The silver bands of her exosuit, clamped close against her scaled skin, reminded him she was anything but.

Sabrina wasn't paying his reptilian companion any attention. Staring blankly at a wall, she shook her head, and said, "Oh God, he really did tell you about the cats, didn't he?"

"Yes."

Her attention snapped back full to him. "How dare you!"

She took a step forward, her expression menacing enough that instinct made him retreat. Her voice was so loud that the dogs stood up in their cage and started barking.

"How dare you feed into his delusion about all this?" she yelled.

"We didn't... I mean..." Len was at a loss, not knowing what to say to calm her down. "He knew about us. He said he'd already told you about us, too."

"He's been making up stories about aliens visiting him since before I was born. That doesn't mean I think they're real!"

"I thought you would believe him. You're family."

She gasped as if he'd struck her. Her eyes widened and her mouth dropped open, a series of strange half-formed sounds coming out.

"Don't you try to play me like that." She jabbed the disabled weapon at him as she spoke. "If he told me the sky was purple, I wouldn't blindly believe him just because he's my grandpa and I love him. And I sure as heck wouldn't encourage him to keep thinking that was the truth."

"Actually, I've seen some sunsets that—"

She let out a frustrated shout, just as she threw the weapon at Len's head. Her aim was pretty good. He ducked to avoid it, and it bounced harmlessly off the wall behind him.

"Whoa," he yelled. "Calm down."

She grabbed up the tub of sandlike stuff and threw it as well. He barely managed to dodge that one, and when it hit the wall, it burst open, spilling large granules of...whatever was in it all over the floor.

"Dammit," Sabrina yelled. "Stop ducking!"

"Then stop throwing things at me!"

Glowering worse than an angry Lyrian, Sabrina charged him. Cyan leapt down from the cage she'd been sitting on. She landed on her feet, one arm outstretched, fingers splayed—all pretense of being a "regular lizard" gone. The air in front of them crackled as a translucent wall of ice-blue force manifested in front of them.

The next few seconds were some of the most confusing and terrifying of Len's life. Time seemed to dilate as Sabrina's expression changed from fury to confusion to disbelief.

She tried to stop when she saw Cyan standing before her, but when Sabrina's feet hit the sand-like substance on the ground, she lost her footing and kept sliding forward. Her arms flailed wildly as she scrambled to reverse her forward momentum, twisting around and falling toward the floor.

Cyan quickly dropped the force field, reaching out with both hands in a gesture that looked like she was trying to catch Sabrina remotely with the anti-gravity field generator in her exosuit.

At that exact moment, the dogs let out a stream of high-pitched yelps. Len jumped at the unexpected sound, turning toward its origin instinctively.

So did Cyan.

A loud crack reverberated through the room as Sabrina hit the floor, her head bouncing on the hard tile.

"Oh no." Len scrambled to Sabrina's side. Her eyes were closed, but she was still breathing. "No, no, no."

"I was distracted at the worst possible moment," Cyan said. "I am so sorry."

"Scan her. Is she okay?"

Cyan held her hands above Sabrina's body, running back and forth along the length of her to scan everything.

"She struck her head hard enough to cause damage to the surface area of her brain," Cyan said. "I believe on Earth they call the injury a concussion."

"Her *brain*?" Len yelled. "You have to heal her. Your exosuit can do that, right?"

"I can heal only minor injuries in others, not an organ as intricate as the brain. She needs a regen bed."

"Then we get her to a regen bed."

Cyan's eyes widened. "What?"

"Can I lift her without hurting her more?" Len's stomach was twisted in knots at the thought.

"I believe so, but—"

"We're taking her to the ship." Len slid his arms underneath Sabrina, then stood, holding her slight form against his chest. Now that she wasn't trying to kill him, she looked so frail and defenseless.

He couldn't believe this had happened. But he would do whatever it took to make it right.

"We can not use the shuttle to take her to a hospital," Cyan said. "The Earthlings will see."

"That's not the ship I meant and we're not taking her to a hospital," Len said. "You said she needs a regen bed. We're taking her to the *Reckoning*."

Cyan's eyes widened. "The Florida base would be more familiar to her." Cyan stammered a bit, wringing her hands. "I am uncertain taking her to a Coalition warship is the wisest choice."

"That warship has much more advanced capabilities than the facilities at our Florida base. Unless you'd like me to take her to your Vegan Life Ship?"

Cyan gasped. "The others would not allow that."

"We did this, Cyan," Len said. "We're responsible. We have to help her."

After a moment, Cyan stood straighter and nodded. "Of course, you are correct. I apologize. What can I do?"

Len nodded at the exit. "You can get the door."

Cyan ran ahead of him. They both emerged into the cold night air.

His breath came out as a visible vapor and he pulled Sabrina closer to his chest, trying to keep her warm. "Why the hell didn't the others tell us it was going to be so cold here?"

"It was supposed to be a quick mission. This chain of events is most unfortunate." Cyan crawled up his body and settled herself around his neck again. "I will warm you as best I can."

Warmth flooded down his body from her exosuit.

"That's better." Glancing down at Sabrina, he said, "You're going to be okay. I promise."

He hurried down the dark street toward their cloaked shuttle.

Chapter Three

Light stung Sabrina's eyes through her eyelids. Voices drifted to her from somewhere close by as she slowly woke.

The first voice was familiar—masculine and smooth. "If I'd asked for clearance, would you have let me bring her aboard?"

"No." The second voice was brusque and strangely flat. "And I suspect you predicted my answer and thus chose not to request permission."

Where was she? And who the heck were these guys?

She remembered getting into her jammies for bed. Trying to find her phone. That's right, she'd left it at work, and—

"OMG!" She bolted upright, her head swimming.

The room sort of seemed to be tilting around her, but it was hard to tell. The walls and floors were all white, gleaming and reflecting the light back so strongly it hurt to try to focus on them.

The floor was a nice dark gray, though. And it was getting closer.

"Not again!"

Strong arms grabbed her and pulled her toward a warm, broad chest. Wow, this guy had muscles. She smiled as she turned to thank him, but froze when she saw his face.

"You!" she yelled. "You're the guy who broke into my pet parlor!"

"I did," he said.

"And said mean things about my grandpa."

"I didn't." His brow furrowed.

"Yes, you did. And you encouraged him in thinking aliens...are...real..."

She rubbed her head, remembering his pet iguana. The extremely well-trained iguana, who had jumped in front of him to protect him.

With a force field.

As she stood completely upright.

"I need to sit down," Sabrina said.

She looked around the room again, only to realize that Len was actually holding her up off the floor. He'd caught her as she fell off of...

Her gaze landed on the flat, padded plastic table where she must have been lying. There were several others just like it lined up along the walls.

Two of them had some sort of clear dome covering them. She could see a man and a woman sleeping inside, pale lines of light coursing down their bodies, as if they were being...scanned.

"What is this place?" she murmured.

"This is my med-bay." One of the most gorgeous men she'd ever seen stepped into her field of view.

He had blue eyes and light brown hair that almost brushed his shoulders. Adding in his chiseled features, Summer-worthy tan, and killer smile, and he could have just stepped off a lot in Hollywood. Especially considering his russet T-shirt and cargo shorts.

Didn't anybody know it was Winter?

He was probably an actor. Because this whole thing had to be a trick.

"This is Dane." Len turned a bit so they could talk without Sabrina having to crane her neck to see him. "He's our Chief Medical Officer."

"Right," she said. "And let me guess. This is a spaceship. And you're all aliens."

"That is correct." A third man joined them, standing next to Dane.

Sabrina blinked. Then she blinked again.

The new guy was an identical copy of the first. Well, except for his haircut. And his total lack of a tan.

And the glower.

And, most importantly, the silver catsuit he was wearing.

Like full-on, 50's sci-fi movie silver catsuit. It had the broad belt and everything. He even had one of those wristband thingies that he could undoubtedly use to control the "ship."

He was ridiculously pale, his hair close-cropped, and he had an air of "do not mess with me" that made her almost, *almost* hesitate before saying, "What the heck are you wearing?"

"This is a standard-issue Coalition uniform," he said. "You are on board the warship known as the *Reckoning*."

"Of course I am." She shrugged off a shiver of misgiving at the name. Grandpa had told her stories about an evil Coalition of Planets that repressed their citizens and treated everyone with callous disregard. But those were just stories.

"Let me make another guess." She pushed more snark into her tone to help herself feel better as she addressed Mr. Flat-tone. "You're the captain, right?"

"The rank is commander in our fleet, but you are correct if you mean that I am in charge of the ship," silver-suit guy said. "My name is Marq. With a 'Q'."

"With a 'Q'," she repeated.

This was just too much. Why would they be going to this extreme to trick her? They really had gone all-out with the set design and those extras in the weird sci-fi beds. Part of her wanted to squeal in delight and jump right into the game.

Part of her that she squashed.

It was harder to want to stop the "romance sub-plot" of their story. Being held in Len's arms felt...better than she wanted to admit.

But she still wanted to leave.

"Okay, if you don't mind, I'll just be going." She pushed against Len's chest, but he didn't budge. She glared up at him. "Also, I hate you."

Len chuckled. Her stomach did a little flip at the sound, making her hate it, too.

I don't care if he's cute. I don't care if he has a really great voice. And eyes. And smile. And body. He's a jerk and he's trying to trick me, and he dragged grandpa *into this. And I need to stop falling for it!*

"What's so funny?" she snapped.

Len shook his head. "I'm just relieved that you're yelling at me. Now I know you're okay."

The urge to laugh bubbled up inside her, but she stamped it down ruthlessly and twisted her mouth into a frown instead.

Len just laughed again.

"I don't understand this exchange," Marq said. "Is this an example of sarcasm? Because I'm still struggling with that concept."

Sabrina turned and cast him an incredibly fake smile. "Then you and I will have a great time communicating."

Marq angled his head to the side, his brow furrowed. "How can she smile and glare at me simultaneously?"

Dane clapped Marq on the back, and said, "Earthlings can manifest sarcasm in their expressions as well as their speech."

Marq shook his head as he regarded Sabrina warily. "This individual might be the most confusing sentient I've ever met."

"I'm about to be the most irate 'sentient' you've ever met if Len doesn't put me down," she said.

"Ah, but I have the advantage now," Len said.

Her stomach twisted in a moment's misgiving. It vanished as soon as he added, "There's nothing for you to throw at me. I made sure Dane removed everything in the room that's not fastened to the hull."

"Jerk," she said.

"I don't know what that means, so I'm going to take it as a term of affection." Len smiled at her, and again, she felt her anger weakening. "I think you're a jerk, too."

This time, a laugh burst out of her before she could stop it. Len's expression transformed. The lines around his eyes softened as his features relaxed, and he cast the broadest smile yet at her.

Her breath hitched at the sight. He was gorgeous before, but this smile took it to the next level.

Get a grip, Sabrina.

"Just because I laughed at your joke doesn't mean I like you," she quickly said.

"I know." Len nodded. "It's further evidence of how much you hate me."

She glowered at him. Dammit, he needed to stop being so…likable.

"If you could put our guest back on the exam table." Dane stepped closer and gestured to the bed she had fallen off of.

Sabrina was almost reluctant to let Len go. The situation was still so strange, and as much as she wanted to smack Len, she felt…safe with him.

This is so confusing.

Len set her on the table gently, keeping a hand on her arm to make sure she was steady.

"Earth doesn't have advanced enough technology to properly deal with head trauma like this—mild as it was," Dane said.

"Head trauma?" She reached up and touched the back of her head, then the sides. Nothing was tender and there were no goose-eggs. She chided herself as she remembered this was all an elaborate ruse.

She had fallen, though. And everything went dark afterward.

There was no way she'd hit her head hard enough to knock herself out without feeling it now. Maybe she had passed out from exhaustion or something?

"The regen bed took care of it," Dane said. "You're all better now—and then some."

A door that Sabrina hadn't noticed earlier slid into the wall and two identical women walked in. They both had long brown hair that was pulled up in buns, and vibrant blue eyes. One was wearing normal clothes and the other had on a silver catsuit.

"Len still should have requested clearance before bringing an Earthling aboard," Marq said.

He was glaring at Len. But then, Marq always seemed to be glaring—at least, in the whole five minutes that Sabrina had known him.

Adding the glare to his weirdly flat tone, and their "commander" seemed oddly menacing. Sabrina took a deep breath and reminded herself that this was all an act.

"Ah, but sometimes it's better to ask forgiveness than permission," the woman wearing normal clothes said.

Marq cocked his head to the side. "That is a logical fallacy."

"That is a valid strategy." The woman in the silver catsuit walked up to Marq and stood on her toes to kiss his cheek. For the first time, his features softened, an unmistakable emotion flooding his face. Love.

It was such a change from before, and so genuine, that Sabrina felt a little lump in her throat. She started to lean closer to Len, but stopped when she realized what she was doing.

Len was still standing next to her as she sat on the table, his hand resting on her arm. She was letting him keep it there just in case she had another wave of dizziness. Not because of how warm it was or that she already found his presence strangely comforting when she should still be throwing things at him.

She couldn't get swept away in this...whatever it was. Elaborate prank? But who would go to so much trouble and why?

The woman who was dressed in regular clothes had crossed to Dane. They slid their arms around each other's waists. Even Marq was resting his arm on the first woman's shoulders as she nuzzled against his side—quite the pair, in their matching spacesuits.

Why add the romance angle to the story? Unless it was to make it that much more compelling.

Sabrina had to tamp down a surge of longing at the happy couples before her. She hadn't been asked out on a date in months. But then, she'd already turned down every available guy in Harbor. Or tried to date them, with catastrophic results.

"Let me take another guess." Sabrina fell back on her snark to defend herself. "All of you 'aliens' are actually clones."

Everybody laughed. She didn't feel it was directed at her, but she scowled at them anyway.

"No, we're just twins," the lady in the silver catsuit said. "I'm Caitlin and that's my sister Brigid. We're from Earth."

"Oh, of course." Sabrina nodded, keeping her expression as serious as she could manage. "So then, I suppose the males are all clones. And they've come to Earth seeking mates, right? There's a population imbalance on their home planet?"

Marq stepped forward, suddenly showing an interest in Sabrina keen enough to make her want to flinch. She sat up straighter instead.

"Sorca is the only clone among us," Marq said.

"That we know of." Dane's smile had vanished.

They all looked dead serious—even Len when she glanced up at him. He gave her a reassuring smile and moved closer.

"Sorca is our Chief of Security," Len said.

Marq also came closer, though that wasn't nearly as reassuring. "And she is on a mission to the Cygnian homeworld. A homeworld that faces the very imbalance you describe."

Sabrina rolled her eyes. She couldn't help it.

"Oh, come on!" she said. "'Mars Wants Women'?' That's the oldest trope in the book!"

"It's a classic—and my personal favorite," Caitlin said, rejoining Marq and pointedly wrapping her arms around his elbow. She pulled him back a bit, then smiled at Sabrina and gave an apologetic shrug.

"I prefer the 'headstrong scientist is exploring the universe and stumbles into love' trope, myself," Brigid said.

Dane's brow furrowed briefly. "Couldn't she be a chef?"

They both laughed as if it was a shared joke. Len started brushing his thumb lightly over Sabrina's arm and, again, she felt herself leaning toward him.

No. No way. This is not happening.

Sabrina slid off the table and pulled away when Len tried to reach for her.

"Whatever story you're weaving, I'm not interested," she said, grateful to find she was finally steady on her feet.

The door was still open, and she intended to use it. Len wasn't quite done trying to reel her in, though.

He followed her, saying, "We're going to take you back to Earth, but there are things we have to explain first."

"Save it," she yelled, quickening her pace. She looked back at the hodgepodge bunch over her shoulder, standing in their 'med-bay' and taking her for a fool. "I don't know why you're doing this, but you're never going to trick me into thinking aliens are real."

She turned to run out the door, and ran smack into a wall of…fur.

Really soft fur, covering a huge, white *something* that filled the doorway and grabbed her arms, gently pushing her back into the room.

"Whoa, whoa, careful there," the wall of fur said. "I have a nestling in tow."

A thin tentacle whipped up from some sort of pouch hidden in all that white fluff. It retreated as a giant, three-fingered, blue hand patted the spot.

There were still two hands on Sabrina's arms, so where had that one come from?

Sabrina looked up and up and up until she saw a

wrinkled blue face with bright blue eyes that had sideways pupils like grandpa's goat, Samwise.

That was just how grandpa had described the being she was staring at, her stomach doing flips, her brain reeling, a high-pitched keening in her ears that made her think she might pass out again.

"C…C… Craig?" she croaked.

He lifted yet another hand to her face to brush away the hair that had flopped in front of her eyes—while he still held on to her with two of his other arms. The fourth was wrapped across his middle, where the little tentacle had emerged.

"Sabrina," he said. "Oh, my, how you've grown!"

Chapter Four

"This can't be happening. This can't be happening. This can't be happening."

Len was starting to worry. Sabrina had been repeating the phrase non-stop ever since Craig had entered the room.

"Poor little thing," Craig said. "I think I broke her."

"She's not broken, she's in shock." Len pulled Sabrina away from Craig and led her back to the table, half-supporting her weight. He helped her sit, her eyes never leaving Craig.

"Sabrina," Len said. "Look at me."

"This can't be happening."

"Sabrina!" He dared to cup her face in his hands so he could urge her to look at him.

When her eyes stayed locked on Craig, even though her face was pointed at him, he stepped in close enough that he completely filled her field of vision. "Look at me. Please."

"Len..." She'd never said his name like that. Desperate and pleading.

His heart pounded and his body was flooded with the desire to act. He had the strangest feeling that he would do *anything* to make that pleading note go away.

Why was she having such a strong reaction to Craig? Marvin had told Len and Cyan that he'd prepared Sabrina for this day. Had told her stories so that when the time was right, she could take over helping 'otherworlders' as Marvin called them. He never hinted this might happen.

Until this moment, Len had never seen any sign of bending in the steel of her personality. That she was turning to *him* for help…

Something deep inside him shifted. The feeling that he would do anything for her grew even stronger.

"Len, this can't be real," she whispered.

"It can and it is." He leaned closer. "And it's going to be okay. I promise."

She pinched her eyes shut and shook her head, grabbing his wrists tight. He was afraid she was going to push him away, but she didn't. She was holding onto him for support.

"It won't," she said.

"It will."

"No, you don't get it." When she opened her eyes again, they were glittering with unshed tears. The sight nearly broke him.

He wanted to comfort her. To hold her. To kiss her till she forgot all about whatever was making her so upset.

Where is this coming from?

Sadirians didn't kiss for comfort. They barely kissed at all. He'd never felt the urge until Sabrina.

"I didn't believe him," she said. "My grandpa. We're family, like you said. And I didn't believe him. I didn't stand by him. How can I ever make that right?"

Len's breath rushed out of him as he finally understood. His heart felt leaden in his chest.

She had attacked Len just for suspecting that he'd had a conversation with her grandpa. She was so protective of Marvin, and in her mind, she had failed him. She hadn't defended him when people thought he was making up stories about aliens.

"Sabrina." Len put his arms around her and pulled her against his chest. She grabbed him even tighter, her hands fisting in the back of his shirt.

Huge, furry arms encircled them. Len looked up to see Craig hugging them both, his flat nostrils flaring as he sniffed the air.

"Do you mind?" Len said.

Craig's lips pulled into a huge smile—which, from a Lyrian, was not really reassuring. From that angle, Len could see the rows and rows of sharp, thin teeth in Craig's mouth.

"I just wanted to smell something," Craig said. He leaned back, and added, "I think we need to leave these two alone to *bond*." He winked at Len.

Len's stomach felt like the gravity generators had failed. That emphasis... That wink...

He'd heard that the Lyrians thought they could tell when

a Sadirian and an Earthling were particularly suited to each other through their scents somehow. Was he saying that Len and Sabrina were a natural pair?

"Bond?" Len said, his mind filling with even more questions. "You don't mean—"

Craig reached out with one of his hands and ruffled Len's hair. "You'll figure it out," Craig said. "Come on, everyone. Let's give them a moment."

Craig herded everyone toward the exit, though Marq was protesting. Caitlin helped drag the commander out. She gave Len an encouraging smile before the door slid shut.

"They're gone now," Len said, keeping his voice as gentle as he could. "It's just us."

Sabrina kept clinging to him. He wasn't sure what to do, but found himself rubbing her back in slow circles.

"Hww cd mh nt bwv m?" Her face was pressed so tight against his chest that he couldn't understand her words.

He didn't want to let her move away, but also needed more information if he was going to truly help. He shifted closer and rested his cheek against her head, keeping them as close as he could.

"What was that?" he asked.

She turned her face slightly to the side. "How could I have not believed him?"

Len chuckled softly. "Very easily, if you're like most Earthlings."

"I don't want to be like most Earthlings."

"You aren't."

She shifted back a bit, glaring up at him, but kept her grip on the back of his shirt. "You just said I was."

Damn. He'd stepped in it again.

"Okay, I *implied* that you were, but just in this one teeny, tiny area," he said.

She narrowed her eyes at him briefly, but then scowled and looked down again. He let out a breath he hadn't known he was holding.

He'd never met a sentient who was as full of fire as Sabrina. Talking to her was challenging, exhilarating.

Holding her was even better.

"I can't believe..." Her voice trailed off, then she gestured toward the door. "That *thing*..."

"That *Lyrian*."

"I'm sorry." She sniffed and nodded. "You're right. That Lyrian. Craig. Oh my God, *Craig*."

She looked up at the ceiling, blinking rapidly as if clearing her eyes. She sniffed again after a moment, then stared at the door.

"He's real," she said.

"Yes."

Finally, she looked back at Len.

"And you're real, too."

Len chuckled. "Last time I checked."

She scowled, and the sight didn't scare him, for once. She was prickly. She was possessive. And he couldn't imagine what it would feel like to have all that fire defending him instead of keeping him away.

He wanted her passion.

His hands were on the sides of her face. He didn't remember putting them there.

The scowl was gone.

"All of this…" she whispered, their faces close enough that he felt her breath warm on his skin.

"Is real. All of it."

What would it feel like to press their lips together? To feel her warmth from even closer, and feed her his own.

Their lips were millimeters away when a voice broke into the moment.

"Um, so, I just woke up from stasis."

Sabrina lurched back, turning toward the regen beds. One of the domes had opened and Xan was sitting up, staring at them.

"Shouldn't there be a med-tech in here to check my stats?" Xan said.

"You're fine," Len snapped.

Xan arched an eyebrow. "You're a science officer, not a med-tech."

"That's what regen beds are for," Len said. "Fixing people."

"I'd rather hear it from Orin or—"

Len cut him off. "Don't you have a ship to navigate?"

Xan's lips twitched up on one side briefly. He quickly

made his expression more serious again. "My shift's not for another standard Earth hour."

"I should go," Sabrina said.

"What? No." Len shook his head.

"I need to get back to Earth." She rolled her eyes, then covered her face with her hands. "I can't believe I just said that."

"This is a lot to process and—" he stopped as the feeling of being watched grew. Turning, Xan was still staring at the pair, openly smiling now, arms crossed and legs kicking under the table.

"Do you mind?" Len said.

"Me?" Xan pointed at his chest, his eyebrows rising comically. He made an overly thoughtful face, then shook his head. "Not at all."

His grin only made Len angrier. They had been having a moment, and then it was ruined.

"Nice to know you guys have smart-alecks, too," Sabrina said.

"What's a smart-aleck?" Xan asked.

She cocked her head. "You have a mirror?"

Xan laughed, then turned to Len. "I like her. Does she have a twin?"

"*She* does not." Sabrina slid to her feet, shaking off Len's hand as he sought to steady her. She faced Xan with her own arms crossed over her chest and glared at him. "And *she* doesn't like being talked about as if she's not in the room."

"Stars, Len." Xan shook his head. "You're luckier than a parcel in a nestling's pouch."

Sabrina turned toward Len and asked, "What does that even mean?"

"Parcels are little furry animals that Lyrians keep as pets," Len said.

Xan let out a laugh. "What it means is that Len has obviously already... What do you Earthlings say? 'Called dibs'."

Chapter Five

"Dibs?" Sabrina pushed as much ire as she could into the word.

"I don't know who Dibs is," Len said, "but I assure you that I have never called them."

She wanted to set them both straight, but when she opened her mouth to give them heck, all that came out was laughter. Her first thought was that she was too tired to resist the strangeness of the situation, but then she realized that she actually felt...better.

The fog of fatigue that had plagued her for the last few days was gone, as were the aches and pains from all the extra work. She thought back to what Dane had said about fixing her concussion "and then some."

"What exactly do regen beds do?" she asked.

Xan shrugged. "They fix people. Just ask our Chief Science Officer."

Len scowled at him, stepping between Xan and Sabrina. "I can go into more detail if you'd like, but the simple answer is that it scans your body for anomalies and corrects them using a variety of different technologies."

"What kind of anomalies?" she said.

"Only those that are deemed dangerous," he said. "Evelyn—she's also an Earthling—taught us that."

A zing of something unpleasant coursed through Sabrina. Something she had no business feeling toward this guy—this *alien*.

She tried to keep her voice neutral as she asked, "Who's Evelyn?"

Xan snickered. Sabrina cast the most baleful stare she could muster at him.

"And that's my cue to leave." Xan jumped off the "regen bed" and headed toward the door. He looked back at them before exiting, and said, "Good luck with that one, Len. You're going to need it."

"What's that supposed to mean?" she shouted, but the door had already closed.

"Sabrina." Len's voice was a calm counterpoint to her own. He rested his hands on her arms and turned her around.

"That guy is an ass."

Len chuckled. "I can't argue with you there."

She shook her head and turned back to him, arms crossed. "So...Evelyn?"

Sabrina was only interested in hearing more about what her fellow Earthlings had been through with these guys— *not* how any "Earth women" might have interacted with Len.

Keep telling yourself that.

"You don't have to worry," he said. "We learned our lesson with the first Earthling we put in a regen bed."

"What happened?"

"The regen bed altered her body so that it was within acceptable parameters. Parameters set for us."

"Oh my God. Is she okay? Did it turn her into one of you?"

Len chuckled again. "No, nothing like that. And we're already genetically almost identical. But Evelyn was terribly nearsighted and always wore these big glasses. The regen bed fixed her eyesight."

Sabrina felt her eyebrows rise. "And that was a problem?"

"From what I heard, she was upset that it messed up her 'nerdgirl street cred'. But I have no idea what that means."

"I get it." Sabrina nodded. "My best friend, Kimmy, wears big glasses and refuses to wear contacts. She doesn't love that she needs them, but at the same time, it's part of her identity."

"No one thought to ask Evelyn before altering her."

"Oh, wow," Sabrina said. "That absolutely sucks."

"It was a big mistake, and one we regret. We're still learning. Being with Earthlings is… It's a big learning curve for us."

"But you've been to Earth before. I mean, grandpa told everyone about Craig visiting for years."

Until the teasing at school had become too terrible for Sabrina and he'd stopped. That had only made people tease him more, though.

"What's Craig up to?" people had said. *"Heard from your friend with the four arms lately?"*

"Actually, all of those interactions were illegal. Earth has preservation status. No one was supposed to visit it without permission from the High Council." Len let out another laugh. "In fact, until recently, Craig was one of the most wanted criminals in the Coalition of Planets."

"You're kidding."

"No. He and his mate, Barbara, ran the most successful smuggling operation in the galaxy. From what Craig told us, Marvin was one of his best sources."

"No way. That's…"

She thought through the stories grandpa had told her about Craig, trying to reconcile them with this new information. Craig had gotten grandpa out of a few scrapes, and apparently they went for walks in the woods together a lot.

Grandpa was always putting things aside for Craig. She remembered helping out in the garden every Spring, and grandpa telling her not to mess with the huge piles of extra seed packets that he'd purchased for Craig.

"Grandpa used to gather seeds," she said. "And… And compost. He even called it 'Craig's compost pile'. But why would anyone want seeds and compost? This is too weird."

"Not when you consider how many planets the High Council stripped completely bare of resources. Almost everyone lives in barren dome worlds or on space stations now. Most of our systems can't even grow their own food."

"Why would the High Council do that?"

"I don't know." He shook his head. "To maintain control? They did everything they could to keep us all completely dependent on them. Craig and Barbara worked to restore ecosystems."

"That's terrible and amazing and...and... I want to help."

Len smiled, little crinkles appearing in the corners of his eyes that made her heart beat faster.

"Of course, you do," he said.

They were standing really close. It was hard for her to focus, especially when she thought about how they had almost kissed before.

Now, they were alone again. Well, except for the lady sleeping in the regen bed. Who could apparently wake up at any moment.

"I'm very sorry for everything that's happened," Len said.

"I'm not."

His brow furrowed, but he waited patiently for her to explain.

"I needed to know about all this," she said. "That it's real. And there's so much more to it than grandpa even shared."

"I'm still sorry you were hurt."

Sabrina shrugged. "I'm better now."

Her mind started racing with ideas for using part of the pet parlor's profits to buy more seeds. Maybe they could do a charity event to raise money.

She shook her head at the thought. How would she explain their cause? Everyone would think she was crazy if she told the truth—like grandpa always had.

"I need to apologize," she said.

"You don't need to apologize to me."

"What?" She shoved his shoulder lightly and laughed. "Not to you. To my grandpa. Can you take me back?"

"Of course."

"I'll have questions along the way."

"I'd be disappointed if you didn't."

She smiled up at him. He hadn't stepped away when she'd pushed him. If anything, he was standing closer now.

"You are unlike any sentient I've ever met before," he said.

"I could say the same thing about you."

"Really?" He cocked his head to the side, as if considering her words.

"For one thing, you've put up with me longer than anyone else. Except Kimmy."

Her chest tightened as she realized what she'd said. She hadn't meant to share something so personal, even if it was true. She held her breath as she waited to see how he'd respond.

He kept having that thoughtful expression, nodding slightly. She'd given him a perfect out if he wanted it— bringing her nuclear snark levels to his attention.

Finally, he spoke.

"Earth must be populated by idiots, then," he said.

She laughed, tension flowing out of her. Something about Len made her feel...safe. It was strange and new and kind of wonderful.

He laced their fingers together, standing close and deepening that feeling of connection that was so new to her.

"I know I can be...a lot," she said, testing the waters further.

"A lot of what?"

If he was going to be scared off, she wanted it to happen now and not after she'd really fallen for him.

Not that she was falling for him at all. That would be insane on many levels.

"Anger?" she offered. "Volatility? Emotion in general?" She shook her head. "Growing up with everyone making fun of me and grandpa for believing in aliens was hard. I mean, Harbor has a lot of... I guess I can't call them crackpots anymore and I shouldn't have in the first place. But grandpa is the most open about it. People still ask him 'How's Craig?' at the grocery store, and he just answers like they're asking about any friend."

"Aren't they?" Len said.

"I guess." She let out an exasperated sigh. "I don't know if it makes me feel better or worse knowing that everything he's told me is real. But I do feel bad for trying to electrocute you."

Len laughed, his lips curving in a broad smile. "You were protecting your loved ones. You call it 'anger' and 'volatility', but I prefer to think of it as passion. And that's something...I have truly longed for."

She felt her cheeks heat again, but it actually didn't bother her. "Well, you'll get plenty of it from me."

His expression softened. "I certainly hope so."

Chapter Six

Biological compatibility aside, Len was starting to see how he and Sabrina could absolutely be an excellent match. She was fire and chaos—constantly surprising him, giving him things to think about. He would never be bored with her.

And he'd finally have someone to share feelings with. To actually *experience* feelings with, together. He loved the feel of her hands in his, their fingers entwined.

"You really must not get out much if you're so intrigued by my emotions," Sabrina said.

Len laughed. "I've been assigned to the *Reckoning* ever since I completed my mental programming and simulation training."

"Are you a soldier or something?"

"Sort of. As Chief Science Officer, I don't see much combat, which is fine with me. I'm brought in mostly to offer advice on weaknesses and to assess the aftermath of our assignments."

"Gee, that sounds like fun." She frowned deeply as she said the words.

Len laughed again. "You're going to have to watch the sarcasm with Marq. He really doesn't get it."

"Yeah, what's up with that guy? He was like a robot until that woman…Caitlin showed up."

"More than you know." Len debated how much to share. It wasn't in his nature to conceal knowledge, and he loved having someone to talk to. "Many of the soldiers on this ship went through mental programming that suppressed their emotions. Marq was one of them."

Sabrina let out a little gasp. "Why would they do that?"

"In some cases, it wasn't voluntary."

Her eyes narrowed and her lips pinched together tight. Len was suddenly glad they'd left her electrocution weapon behind at the pet parlor. She looked ready to use it.

"We're working on reversing the procedure," Len said. "For those who want to. But in the meantime, you should go easy on him. He's not familiar enough with the emotions needed to pick up on sarcasm."

She shook her head. "I sometimes wish I could control my temper better. Maybe not take things so personally. But the thought of not having any emotions at all…"

"It's not quite that bad. The process had varying levels of success with different people. And many did volunteer for it."

"Why?"

"Our lives have been…" He struggled to find the right words. "Nothing was really in our control. We only realized just how little influence we had after General Serath, our new leader, visited Earth."

"Did he stage a coup or something?"

Len cocked his head at her. The translation session he'd undergone for her language wasn't quite able to convey the meaning of her words. She must have picked up on his confusion, because she explained.

"Did he take over after he found out what the previous leaders were doing?" she said.

"No, he didn't take over. The High Council was destroyed, along with our homeworld. The entire system, actually."

"That's awful. What happened?"

"Our people are at war." He tried not to think too hard on the battle that had ended Sadr-4. "My people, I should say. We're trying to keep Earth out of it as much as possible."

"Thanks, I guess. And I'm sorry." She squeezed his hand.

"Earth's Department of Homeworld Security has been very welcoming."

"I'm sorry, the Department of what now?"

"It's a secret organization at the moment. But they've been helping some of us relocate to the Sol system. Helping us build domeworlds and a space station."

"It's hard to believe that we're helping you. You're the ones with the regen beds."

"And you're the ones with the Vegans."

She arched an eyebrow at him.

"Remember Cyan?" he said.

Her gaze became unfocused and she shook her head. "The little lizard lady that almost killed me? How could I forget."

"She didn't almost kill you. That was all an accident."

"Tell that to my concussion."

"I can't, because we healed it." He smiled, hoping she would laugh, but she just scowled at him. He cleared his throat and looked away. "Cyan is a Vegan. They've settled on Earth and claim it as their home."

"Are *they* trying to take over?"

"Not at all. The arrangement was in part to protect Earth from the war. There's no way anyone would take you on with the Vegans as your allies. Their technology is the most advanced in the galaxy."

"Well, that's cool, I guess."

"It's very cool. And since almost a dozen Sadirians have pair-bonded with Earthlings, we're hoping to solidify our own alliance with you."

"So, you're a Sadirian."

"Yes." He shook his head. "I'm probably not explaining this well enough and this is kind of a core dump."

"It's a lot to take in." After a pause, she said, "And pretty scary, honestly."

Len didn't want to scare her. He wanted her to feel the

same sort of wonder that he felt when he looked at her, listened to her, tried to predict what she would say or do next.

"I want to show you something," he said.

She frowned, eyebrows lowering. But he thought he saw a hint of a smile on her lips.

"Come on," he said. "You'll love it."

"That's what they all say."

He wasn't sure what she meant, but laughed anyway. She smiled in return.

Keeping his hold on one of her hands, he led her out into the hallway. They passed through several corridors, moving closer to the outer hull of the ship.

"You know, this would be a lot less awkward if I wasn't in my pajamas," she said.

"What are pajamas?"

She laughed briefly, but her smile faded when she saw that he didn't join in. "Wait, you're serious?"

"Our cultural programming sessions covered most of the basics, but there are still many areas that we're unclear on. Especially if we don't have an equivalent for an Earth concept."

"You have to have pajamas. The clothes you sleep in?"

"We sleep in our uniforms."

She was pensive for a moment, then said, "Those silver catsuits?"

"Yes."

"That sounds awful. Do you at least have blankets? Pillows?"

"Caitlin has begun introducing us to those things, though most of us still sleep in our regen beds."

"You sleep in those clear-topped beds in the med-bay?" Sabrina said.

"Not in the med-bay. We have one in each of our quarters."

"Oh my God. Do they close while you sleep in them?"

"Of course they do. How else would they regenerate our bodies?"

She shuddered and shifted a little closer to him as they walked. He wasn't sure what was upsetting her about the idea, but had to admit that he was enjoying her proximity.

"Since we're working to better understand each other," he said, "why do you Earthlings keep calling our uniforms 'catsuits'? I've seen cats, and our uniforms look nothing like them."

Sabrina laughed. "We call them catsuits because... Well, they're tight and form-fitting and... Honestly, I'm not sure where the term came from."

Len smiled at her. "Then I guess we have that in common."

They had arrived at the outer hull. He led her to one of the inactive viewports, his heart racing strangely.

While dormant, the viewport looked like the rest of the hull—smooth, white, and featureless. But once it was activated, showing the view beyond... Well, he hoped it would be an experience she would never forget.

He'd never been around someone as unpredictable as Sabrina. It was both fascinating and frightening, given her temper. He hoped she would like this surprise.

"Why are we staring at a blank wall?" she said, after glancing back and forth from his gaze to the viewport.

"It's not a wall," he said.

He pressed the control to activate the viewport, his chest tight with anticipation.

Chapter Seven

Sabrina didn't know what Len was planning, but she could tell he was up to something. That smirk of his was firmly in place. She was starting to like it.

He nodded toward the wall, then tapped it, his smile growing. She followed his gaze.

Her heart lurched in her chest.

The wall had vanished, leaving nothing but the vacuum of space beyond. She leapt toward Len, grabbing his arm and trying to pull him away from the gaping hole.

They stumbled back a few steps before he caught her up against his chest. Everything was spinning again.

"Relax," he said. "It's just a viewport."

"Oh."

Duh.

Of course it was. As if he would jettison them both into space.

"I'm sorry." He held her closer.

She looked up to say something snarky, but the concern etched into his features made the words catch in her throat. Her heart started hammering for a completely different reason.

"I would never do anything to hurt you." He dusted a bit of hair back from her forehead, tucking it behind her ear. "I just... I wanted to share this with you. I didn't think it would frighten you."

"It didn't. I mean... The *whole wall* disappeared. But it only startled me."

His lips twitched at the edges, as if he was trying to stop a smirk from happening. He nodded solemnly. "Of course."

She narrowed her eyes at him and scowled, pushing away from his chest. But her hands caught his, seemingly on their own, and tugged him after her.

It was just because she was still a little freaked out. Not at all because she liked the way his hands felt in hers.

The viewport was huge. Disorienting from its sheer size. And it was completely clear.

She inched forward when she was close, reaching out with one hand while keeping a tight grip on Len's with the other. Something solid met her fingertips.

"What is this?" she asked.

"It's one of our larger viewports. What you're seeing is actually a projection of the space outside. I... I've always loved the view. I thought you might enjoy it as well."

"I do. I am."

She shook her head, an odd lump forming in her throat that made it hard to form words. She finally let go of his hand and pressed both of hers against the surface, leaning as close to it as she could to view the vast expanse surrounding them.

Darkness and stars. So many stars. Even more than she could see when she and grandpa used to go out to the countryside with the telescope when she was a kid and still believed all his stories.

Len messed with his watch, and suddenly, the view changed. Sabrina gasped, taking in the new vista. The far side of the moon dominated the viewscreen, with Earth visible beyond.

She hadn't seen many pictures of the moon from this angle, but was pretty sure they never included what looked like a domed city filled with lush greenery and a lake large enough that she could see its sparkling blue water. There was also a double-dome site near it with two spiraling pillars shooting up from depths she couldn't see the bottom of, glittering lights moving up and down along their surfaces.

Small shuttles flew out from the moon's surface, heading back and forth between a skeletal structure orbiting it that was undoubtedly the start of a magnificent space station.

Her knees started to wobble, her eyes filling with tears. Len stepped closer, his chest brushing her back. She leaned into him and he wrapped his arms around her, but thankfully didn't say anything. They stood that way in silence as she processed everything she was seeing.

"I've dreamt of this my entire life," she whispered.

"Really?"

"Grandpa told me stories. Things that Craig had shared. The vapor pits of Scorpii-prime. The crystal homeworld of the Cygnians."

"I thought you didn't believe in aliens."

"I'm talking about before the teasing. Before I grew up and became too old to believe. But this... This is magic," she said.

"Actually, it's technology."

She didn't know whether to smack him or kiss him for lightening the mood. She decided to give him a menacing glare.

"You know what I mean." She half-turned in his arms. Which meant they were face-to-face. Her glare faltered.

He was much taller than she was, but he was also leaning close. His warm breath fanned her face.

"Oh, I absolutely know what you mean," he said. "This is the best kind of magic."

He closed the distance between them, pressing his lips to hers.

She gasped at the fire that raced through her body from the moment of contact, lighting her up all the way to her toes. The moment her lips parted, he slid his tongue between them, tasting and exploring her.

Her knees went weak. Her stupid knees went weak. And she couldn't even blame them.

She reached up and grabbed the back of his neck to keep herself upright. Not at all because she wanted to see how soft his hair felt as it slid between her fingers. Her mind conjured up images of things he could be doing to other parts of her with that nimble tongue of his, her fingers buried in his hair.

As if he could read her mind—or sense her need—he slid his hands down to her backside and lifted her up. She wrapped her legs around his waist, plundering his mouth as soundly as he'd done to hers.

With a groan, he pressed them against the viewport, grinding his erection against her core. Sparks were going off behind her eyelids.

He worked his way to her neck, sucking and biting the sensitive skin just under her ear. His fingertips dug into her as he pressed against her harder and faster and—

Someone cleared their throat, loudly, a few feet away. Len placed his arm against the viewport, as if shielding her from the gazes of whoever was interrupting them. She was so lost in the clouds of lust they'd gathered, she barely cared if they had an audience.

Until she saw them.

Her hands stiffened on the back of Len's neck. She willed him closer, not daring to move herself.

"Len," she whispered. "Do you see the giant ant-people?"

"Yes, I do," he said.

She let out a relieved breath. "Good. It's not just me, then."

Craig was standing between them—two enormous ants, standing on their back legs. They were almost Sabrina's size, maybe five feet tall. Their bodies had a thorax and abdomen, with a narrow waist linking them. Grapefruit-sized, segmented eyes dominated their heads, which were as big as watermelons, resting on their thin necks. Their antennae twitched as they stared at her, their multi-segmented eyes strobing in various shades of pink.

"Ant-people," she murmured.

Len leaned in and whispered, "Antareans."

"Oh, right…" She remembered grandpa talking about Antareans, and how kind and gentle they were.

"And they have very sensitive hearing," Len said.

The taller Antarean lifted one of her many, many arms, and said, "We also have very keen scent vents, capable of discerning a vast array of—" she cleared her throat and looked up at the ceiling "—pheromones."

"Meaning, you two should get a room!" Craig put one set of hands on his hips, the other arms busy with the nestling wriggling in his…pouch. "What would Marvin say if he knew you two were out here practically mating against a viewport."

"I'm sorry." She pushed against Len, and he backed away enough to let her down. He held onto her though, which was good, since her knees were still a little weak.

"I really am sorry," she said. "For so many things. I need to tell grandpa." She looked up at Len. "Can you take me back? I need to talk to him."

Len looked over her shoulder at the viewport. He tapped a few commands, then frowned, a deep furrow appearing between his eyebrows.

"What is it?" Sabrina looked over her shoulder at the view and gasped.

Earth filled the viewport, land masses painted pale brown and green amid oceans gleaming blue. Bright white clouds swirled across its surface. Her throat felt tight and she had to wipe her eyes to clear them.

"It's so beautiful," she said.

"It is." There was a long pause before Len added, "But I can't take you back."

Chapter Eight

"What did you say?"

The wistful expression in Sabrina's face had vanished to be replaced with the much more familiar anger. Len swallowed hard, wanting to see that softness from her again, but knowing it was highly unlikely to happen. At least, in the near future.

"I can't take you back." He quickly added, "Yet."

"Why not?"

"Our cloaking devices aren't perfect." Len gestured to the viewport. "It's the middle of the day in Harbor right now. Protocols forbid us from traveling to the surface when Earthlings are more likely to see—"

"Wait, the middle of the day?" Her voice rose as she spoke. She shook her head, staring back at the viewport. "Oh, no, no, no."

"What's wrong?" he said.

She locked her gaze on him again, and he could feel the fire in them. Not nearly as pleasant as the heat they'd generated just a few moments ago.

"Do you have any idea how worried my family will be

about me?" she said. "And Kimmy? Oh God, we left the parlor such a mess! They're going to think you killed me."

"But I didn't." The idea was so upsetting, he couldn't even let the statement pass. "I saved you."

She crossed her arms and glared at him.

"I mean, I helped you," he said.

She raised her eyebrows.

"After…" he began, "you know…"

Craig let out a huff of breath. "'Elders watch their feet near you.' Come on, Sabrina. I can take you home."

Sabrina smirked at Len, then straightened her pajamas and walked over to Craig. She nodded stiffly at the Antareans, who bowed in return before hurrying down the hallway past Len. They were making a chittering sound that sounded suspiciously like giggling.

Len chased after Sabrina as she and Craig headed for the hangar bay. "Wait, you can't."

"What, because of 'Sadirian protocols'?" Craig made air quotes with two of his hands as he said the last two words. He snorted. "Please."

"Not because of the protocols," Len said. "Think of what would happen if Earthlings saw your ship."

Craig stopped so quickly that Len bounced off the Lyrian's back. As he stumbled, Sabrina reached out to help him regain his balance.

Craig towered over them both, jabbing a finger in Len's direction.

"That's just offensive," Craig said. "Barbara and I were the best smugglers in the galaxy. For the last three-hundred years, no Sadirian vessel has ever been able to catch the faintest whiff of our scent—and it wasn't for lack of trying."

One of the nestling's tentacles managed to elude Craig's grip and started pointing at Len in an approximation of Craig's earlier gesture. Sabrina inched closer to Len, holding his arm tight.

"That's *almost* cute…" she whispered.

"Almost." He nodded as subtly as he could manage.

Craig let out another huge puff of breath, then pushed the nestling's appendage back in his pouch.

"My point is," he grunted as the nestling struggled against his efforts. "If you couldn't detect us with all your precious technology, there's no way anything the Earthlings have will see us."

Three hands resting on his belly, he glared at Len, as if challenging him to disagree.

"I… You…" Len began.

"You do seem a little distracted," Sabrina said.

Len could have kissed her again, for coming to his aid. And just because he liked kissing her.

"Stop that." Craig spoke pointedly to Len, shaking his head and snorting out a breath. "Antareans aren't the only one with sensitive 'scent vents', and you're stinking up the corridor with your pheromones." He turned to Sabrina, and added, "It's nothing I can't handle."

"Then what are we waiting for?" Sabrina said. "Let's get me home."

Craig nodded, then turned and marched down the corridor. Sabrina started to follow, releasing Len's arm. He caught her hand in his.

"Sabrina…"

She glanced at their hands, but didn't pull away. "My family needs to know I'm okay."

"We can contact them. Simulate your communication technique."

"This all started because I left my phone at work. They've probably already found it by now—and my stun-gun—in the middle of that mess."

Len really didn't know how to deal with that.

"I'm going back now," Sabrina said. "With or without you."

Len swallowed hard. "The commander is going to vaporize me for this."

Sabrina actually paled. "That Marq guy? He wouldn't really—"

"No, it's just an expression." Len felt a smile tug at his lips. "But thanks for caring."

Her glare returned full-force, the impact hitting him in the chest and making his smile broaden.

"Then what are we waiting for?" she said.

"Apparently, you're waiting for me to shove you both in

my pouch and carry you to my ship," Craig shouted. "I thought you were in a hurry."

The nestling managed to get two tentacles out and waved them in the air as if the idea of having company excited her. Craig grabbed the flailing limbs and tucked them back into the pouch.

"Sorry." Sabrina turned and hurried toward Craig, pulling Len after her. She kept a tight grip on his hand.

With Craig's enormous height, they had to jog to keep up with his pace. They quickly reached the small hangar bay dedicated to the Lyrians' ship. Craig keyed in a special access code that Marq had set up for them.

If the previous commander were still in charge of the *Reckoning,* Craig and Barbara would be on the other side of a very different security system—one designed to keep them prisoner. Now, they were honored guests.

It seemed impossible that so much had changed in such a short amount of time. But then, Len looked down at Sabrina, her eyes wide as she waited for the door to open, her hand holding onto his tightly, and he realized that reality could change in an instant. Sabrina was in his life, and everything was different now.

"Come along," Craig said.

"I don't understand." Sabrina glanced all around the seemingly empty space. "Where's your ship?"

Craig chuckled. "Exactly."

He lifted a hand and started tapping a sequence on the

hull of his cloaked ship. A large rectangle appeared as the hatch opened, a ramp descending to give them easy access to the ship.

"That is so cool," Sabrina murmured.

She followed Craig onto the ship, still holding Len's hand. He was grateful for it. He hadn't been aboard the Lyrian vessel himself.

"Is...um..." he began, "Is Barbara here?"

"No, she is not," Craig said. "No need to worry."

"Why would you worry about Barbara?" Sabrina asked.

Len wasn't sure how to answer without offending Craig. "She has a reputation for having very strong opinions."

Craig laughed. "She has a reputation for having very strong arms—and a tendency to use them to rip apart people she doesn't like. Just ask Zemanni."

"Zemanni?" she asked.

"He's a member of the Department of Homeworld Security now, but started off as an assassin," Len said.

"He's just lucky he's such an extremely skilled shapeshifter." Craig snorted. "Otherwise, he'd never have been able to piece himself together when she was done with him."

"You're kidding, right?" Sabrina looked back and forth between Craig and Len. "Right?"

"We should really go," Len said, dodging the question.

Craig rolled his eyes and slammed a fist against a control panel. The hatch closed behind them.

Len's heart was hammering in his chest as they walked down a broad hallway. They might be on the same side now, but Barbara also had a reputation for hating Sadirians. She'd mellowed on the issue now that her adopted human son had pair-bonded with Vay, their Chief Cultural Programmer—no, *Liaison*, now—and they were all working together, but still...

"This is so cool." Sabrina was staring all around at what must be the ship's command center.

Len had been too busy watching for Barbara. Now that he took a moment to look around, he shared Sabrina's wonder.

The ceilings were higher than the *Reckoning's* bridge, but then, Lyrians were over two feet taller than the average Sadirian. Most of the metal surfaces had a pale blue cast to them, and shimmered from light sources Len couldn't detect.

There were four huge chairs spread through the space, each near a section of wall covered with control panels. A long, wide bench took up the center of the room. The captain's chair?

Craig sat in one of the chairs, two of his hands working the controls. He gestured with a third toward one of the other seats.

"Strap in, since our Sadirian friend is so concerned with protocols." He turned to them and patted the arm of his chair affectionately. "Besides, she's got a bit of a kick to her."

"Let's do as he says." Len steered Sabrina toward one of the seats. He pulled the harness over her body, tightening the straps as much as he could. There was still way too much space for it to be effective at all.

"Two per seat, Len," Craig said. "Otherwise, your tiny bodies will be sliding all over the place."

Len looked down at Sabrina. Her lips were in a thin line and her brow was furrowed. If he didn't know better, he'd swear she was nervous. Honestly, so was he.

The idea of sitting next to her took the edge off, though.

She scooted over as he joined her. The seat suddenly didn't seem so huge. With the two of them scrunched in together, it was downright cozy.

He quickly figured out how to get the straps over them both in a way that seemed like it would at least keep them in the chair without inflicting serious damage if they hit some turbulence. He doubted it would help in a crash, but hopefully that wouldn't be an issue.

This time, he was the one who reached for Sabrina's hand. Again, she didn't pull away. She was staring intently out the viewport.

Craig had already opened the hangar bay door. Something beeped as he deactivated the forcefield between them and the void of space.

Sabrina's grip tightened.

"It's okay," Len said.

She nodded tersely, leaning closer into his side. Since they were already pretty much tied together in the chair, he let go of her hand and wrapped his arm around her instead. She blew out a small breath and rested her hand on Len's thigh, relaxing against him.

The motion did anything but relax him. What felt like currents of electricity shot up his leg, right to his groin. His chest tightened, the hairs on his skin rose. He wanted to kiss her again.

"Seriously?" Craig covered his nose with one hand. His voice had a nasal pitch to it as he continued. "You're worried about the nestling distracting me while you've got *that* going on?"

"It's a physiological response," Len half-shouted.

"What is?" Sabrina finally pulled her gaze away from the viewport. She stared up at Len, their faces close. Stars, she was beautiful.

Len swallowed hard, then lifted her grip from his thigh with his free hand and interlaced their fingers.

"Oh," she said.

It was getting easier to tell when she was hiding a smile. That, or she was getting worse at suppressing it.

He hugged her closer.

The ship lifted off of the hangar bay floor, hovering for a moment before zipping out into space. Sabrina gasped and reached over to clutch at Len's shirt.

Craig did a quick spiral around the *Reckoning*. Even

though the artificial gravity kept them firmly in their seats, the visual perspective of spinning upside-down and right-side-up so quickly made Len dizzy. Sabrina held him tighter, and he suddenly didn't mind.

They leveled out as they passed the framework for space station *Outreach*, then banked sharply, bringing Earth into view. Sabrina gasped again, leaning forward in her seat as far as the restraints would allow.

She didn't say anything, but squeezed his hand almost painfully tight. When he looked over at her, she was biting her lip and her eyes were filled with tears.

So much passion...

He wished he could give her privacy to process the enormity of what she seemed to be feeling, but strapped together as they were, he didn't have many options. Then she looked up at him and smiled.

It was the first truly unguarded expression he'd seen from her. If he hadn't been strapped into the seat, he might have keeled over from the sight—the softness in eyes that had only ever been laser-sharp as she looked at him.

"I'm going to need to vent the atmosphere to clear things out when you two are done in here," Craig said. "You better tone it down before you get to Marvin's, or he'll have your hides—plain as they are."

Both of their hides? Sabrina must be putting off the same sort of pheromones Craig was complaining about from Len.

"You can always open up the hatches when we land," Len said. "Earth air is so much better than the recycled atmosphere on our ships."

"Speak for yourself, Sadirian," Craig said. "We have a crystalline filtration system from Cygnus-prime. And as for landing, no thank you. Marvin's going to be on a tear if he thinks Sabrina was in danger, and once he sees you together…" Craig shook his head. "He has a shotgun and I don't want to spend the rest of the day picking buckshot out of my pelt."

"Can you call him now so he calms down?" Len asked.

Craig chuckled. "Where's the fun in that?"

"If you can call him, I'd appreciate it," Sabrina said. "I don't want him worrying any longer than necessary."

Craig let out a sigh. "I already tried to call. He's not answering. I think Mariana might be with him."

"That's great." Sabrina leaned forward again to face Craig more fully. "You can introduce yourself to her. She's our sheriff, and everyone loves her. If she sees you, she'll know grandpa isn't crazy and can convince the rest of the town."

Craig swiveled his chair around. His shoulders slumped.

"Oh, sweetie," he said. "If it were that simple, I would have done that decades ago. "Humanity isn't stable enough to find out that the universe is so much fuller than they realize."

"You don't know that," she snapped. At a Lyrian.

Len felt his eyebrows hitch, waiting to see how Craig would react. Before he had a chance, Sabrina went on.

"There's a freaking Department of Homeworld Security," she said. "Humans already know aliens are real, and are interacting with them. Harbor is a perfect place to scale that up."

One of Craig's eyebrow ridges rose. "Scale up?"

"It's a small town," she said. "We're isolated. And even if someone said something about you, no one would believe them."

"That's actually a really good point," Len said.

They'd been talking about building a new town, much like their Kindred colony on the moon, only on Earth. It was supposed to be a place for aliens to visit the planet and serve as a neutral meeting ground during the intra-galactic conflict going on between the Coalition of Planets and the Tau Centauran Assembly.

The biggest problem was how to find people to support the operation. They needed people to help out with the activities of the Department of Homeworld Security, as well as the visiting aliens. And if part of the point was introducing sentients to Earthlings, having the whole town populated by Sadirians wouldn't really help.

"We're already known as the town where people think that aliens are real," Sabrina said. "I mean, I guess where people *know* that..." Her eyes narrowed. "Wait a minute. Is grandpa the only person you've been hanging out with in

Harbor?"

Craig turned back to the viewport quickly. "Oh, look, here we are back at Earth."

Chapter Nine

Sabrina opened her mouth to try to keep Craig from evading the topic, but the words froze as she saw Earth growing larger in the viewport. It was so beautiful.

Clouds swirled past them, the blue of the ocean giving way to greens and browns with features becoming more distinct as they descended toward the ground. Very quickly.

She pressed herself tighter against Len's comforting warmth. He actually relaxed a bit as she snuggled up next to him.

How the heck had she ended up here? Flying to her grandpa's house on an alien smuggler's ship and practically sitting in an alien's lap.

A really cute alien. Who knew how to kiss.

She felt her cheeks prickle, and immediately reined in that train of thought. No sense upsetting Craig with her 'pheromones'. Plus, she didn't like him knowing her business.

She couldn't wait to get out of the ship. The fact that Len would be with her... She liked it more than she wanted to admit.

"Uh, yeah," Craig said. "Mariana's here."

The ship came to an abrupt halt just above the chicken coop in grandpa's backyard. Sabrina expected to be thrown forward against the harness, but again, whatever inertia or...G-forces or whatever they were called that she thought they should feel were being offset somehow.

"That's quite a trick," she said.

"One of an infinite supply." Craig grinned, one hand practically flying over the controls. He spun around in his chair and rose, heading toward the hallway that led to the hatch. "Come along."

"Just a second." Len started fiddling with the harness. He managed to loosen it, but the fastener seemed stuck.

"Here." Sabrina wiggled away from Len, finding enough slack to slide down over the edge of the chair.

She had to turn sideways to manage to get to her knees, bracing herself against Len's thigh to push herself free. She ended up kneeling between his legs.

They stared at each other for what felt like a long moment but she hoped wasn't more than a few seconds. The heat in his gaze warmed her to her toes.

"What's taking so long?" Craig called from somewhere down the hall.

"Coming," Sabrina yelled, her face—and other body parts—flooding with heat. "I mean, just a minute."

She leapt up, then pointed at the chair and said, "You should be able to shimmy out of it now."

"I'm gonna need a minute," Len said.

Sabrina did her best not to stare at the impressive bulge straining the front of his pants. And mostly failed.

"I'll just wait by the hatch," she said. "With Craig."

Craig the space-sasquatch, who was waiting for them and owned this ship and would absolutely not be okay if Sabrina and Len did anything in that really spacious chair.

She backed away a few steps, feeling a pull toward Len beyond inertia or G-forces or anything like that. As soon as she could, she turned and hurried down the hallway. Craig was standing by the open hatch, his chest swelling with each deep breath he took.

"Sorry," Sabrina said. "I didn't mean to stink up your ship."

Craig chuckled, the deep, rumbling sound vibrating through the flooring. "It's not that it's a bad smell," Craig said. "Just... TMI, is what you would say, I believe."

"No kidding." She looked out over grandpa's yard. A couple of chickens were scratching at the ground a few feet below, completely oblivious to the ship floating right above them. Craig hadn't extended the ramp yet.

"I do love your Winters here," Craig said, looking wistfully out the hatch. "It's a shame this one has been so mild. It doesn't seem right to be so warm in these parts this early in the year."

"I remember grandpa telling me how much you love the snow."

"I'll be sure to visit when the nestling is older." Craig rubbed a hand over his pouch. The fur undulated as the nestling moved around inside. "She'll love it, too."

"I'm glad it isn't too cold today," Sabrina said. "Len didn't bring a coat."

Craig rolled his eyes. "What is with these so-called 'adults'? My Henry does the same thing all the time."

Craig tapped on a panel next to the hatch. It opened up, revealing a small compartment. He pulled out a coat that was about Len's size, then handed it to her.

"We always keep these handy now," Craig said. "Just in case. You humans and Sadirians are genetically nearly identical." He made a tsking noise. "Such fragile things."

"Are you sure you can't stay for a visit?" Sabrina asked, folding the coat over her arm. "We need to discuss how to prove to the town that aliens are real. I can try to get Mariana to leave."

"Mariana is more stubborn than a Centauran with an icicle."

She cocked her head to the side, but before she could ask her question, Len appeared at the end of the hallway and Sabrina's thoughts cut off. Goosebumps rose along her arms and the ship suddenly didn't seem to have enough air, even standing right next to the open hatch.

She'd never known someone who could derail her ability to think just by existing.

It wasn't just that he was gorgeous—tall and built, trying

to smooth down his hair with one hand and only messing it up more. The way he looked at her with that open smile of his, the eagerness in his gaze, the intense curiosity without a single drop of judgment. She didn't think she'd ever met a more genuine person.

And he liked her. Temper and all. She hadn't managed to scare him off, and she had to be honest with herself—she'd tried.

He joined them at the hatch, not even giving Craig a second-glance.

She felt a goofy smile spread across her face, and didn't bother trying to hide or change it. For once in her life, she didn't feel like she had to.

"Hi," she said.

"Hi," he said.

"Cygnus X." Craig rolled his eyes, then gave them both a shove strong enough to send them sprawling out of the hatch. "Bye!"

"Hey!" she and Len both yelled.

They landed on a soft pile of hay, but still!

Chickens scattered, clucking loudly in protest at the two people who'd basically fallen from the sky into their enclosure.

Sabrina turned to glare at Craig, and for a moment was stunned to see nothing but blue sky and white clouds above —except for the rectangular opening revealing the four-armed Lyrian and the inside of his ship.

As the hatch started closing, Sabrina rose to her feet, and shouted, "This conversation isn't over!"

The last thing she saw was Craig waving. Then the hatch slid shut, and all she could see was the sky beyond.

"Craig!" she shouted.

"Sabrina?" Mariana's voice was clear and commanding, even from the front of the house. "Is that you?"

Crap.

She wasn't supposed to tell Mariana about Craig. She wasn't supposed to tell anyone. Sabrina finally knew that aliens were real, and was supposed to keep that to herself?

Wheeling around, she said, "This sucks!"

Len had other concerns.

"You're coming back for me, right?" he shouted. "Right?"

He bent down and picked up a small stone, then threw it toward where the ship had been. The stone kept flying.

Craig was gone.

"Shit," Len said.

He started rubbing his arms. It was warm for January, but it was still January. Sabrina held up the coat and helped him into it.

"Thanks," he said.

"Sure."

They were about to have another moment—right there in grandpa's chicken yard. But then grandpa's voice came bellowing out from the house.

"Sabrina!"

"It's me, grandpa." She ran to the gate and undid the wire that acted as a latch, then quickly closed it and wrapped the wire around the gate post again—a habit drilled into her after years of chasing loose chickens.

Grandpa appeared around the side of the house, running full-blast toward her. She kicked up her speed as she ran to him, knowing he wouldn't stop worrying till he could give her a hug.

"There you are." He grabbed her up in a bear hug, lifting her feet from the ground. She clutched him just as hard, fighting back tears again.

All those summers spent on his farm came rushing back. For a moment, she felt the little girl that she'd once been stirring within her—the one who believed.

Grandpa put her back on her feet, but held on to her arms, bending down to look her in the eye. "You had us all scared half to death. Where have you been?"

"Grandpa, I—" She balked as she saw Mariana walking across the yard, an intense gaze on her face. Sabrina turned to see what Mariana was looking at.

Len was still in the chicken yard, messing with the wire that secured the gate. It looked like he was actually making it more secure.

One of the hens was pecking at his shoelace. He glanced down at the bird and flinched, then cautiously tried to nudge her away with his foot.

"Could someone maybe help me figure this thing out?" Len said. One of the chickens let out a loud ca-caw, and Len jumped, covering his head with his arms. "What the hell are these things?"

"They're Plymouth Rocks." Sabrina tried to cover Len's gaff by giving the name of their breed. Of course, he ruined it.

"Rocks?" he said, keeping his hands up above his head as if he thought the chickens might try to eat his fingers. "They look like birds."

Mariana's brow furrowed. A breeze picked up, ruffling a few of the dark hairs that had escaped the tight bun at the base of her neck.

"This guy a friend of yours?" Mariana asked.

"This is Len," Sabrina said. "He's…more than a friend."

That got everyone's attention.

And, impossibly, it was true.

Mariana glanced over at Sabrina briefly before returning her focus to Len.

Grandpa straightened, his chest puffing out as he tucked Sabrina protectively against his side. He was over six feet tall himself, and packed with muscle from a lifetime of hard work.

Len seemed oblivious to the posturing. He cocked his head to the side, as if he was working through some problem.

"More than a friend?" Len said. "What does that mean?"

"Harbor is such a small town." Mariana turned her attention back to Sabrina. "I'm surprised I haven't heard about this till now."

Before Sabrina could think of how to respond, Len said, "How do I get out of this place?" He stepped back, eyeing the fence and the ground surrounding it. "Is there a proximity sensor?"

Sabrina would have smacked her forehead if grandpa wasn't holding onto her so tight. Didn't Len and his fellow aliens get training for this sort of thing?

The furrow on Mariana's forehead deepened. "Could one of you explain why I spent my morning cordoning off Kimmy's pet parlor with crime scene tape?"

"Oh, no." Sabrina gasped. "This is all a misunderstanding."

"Then maybe you can clarify matters for me," Mariana said.

"And maybe someone can get me out of this enclosure?" Len glanced down at another chicken who'd taken an interest in his shoelace. He sidestepped the bird and took a few steps away, but more started following him, clucking softly.

Sabrina almost laughed at the sight. The chickens seemed to like him. She liked him, too.

"Len surprised me." She tried to remember what the room had looked like before she hit her head. "And I spilled some kitty litter."

Do not mention the talking lizard lady.

"And the reason your stun-gun was on the floor?" Mariana asked.

"Like I said, he surprised me." Sabrina looked up at her grandpa. "And you told me to always be prepared."

Grandpa squeezed her a little harder, his mouth almost twitching up into a smile.

"And you didn't answer your phone because?" Mariana asked.

Sabrina shrugged. "I left it at work. I still can't find it."

She hoped that Kimmy had it by now. It felt weird to be walking around without a way to connect with other people or the Internet.

"Okay, then," Mariana said. "But what tore up the metal door on the cat kennel? And what was that weird silver chemical splattered everywhere?"

"Well," Sabrina was set to respond, but halted abruptly as she realized she had no idea what Mariana was talking about. "Wait, what?"

"Silver chemical?" Len asked, walking backwards this time, and alternating his gaze between the humans and the chickens following him. "What kind of..." he leapt over an overly-curious hen, "chemical?"

"If I knew that, I wouldn't be asking Sabrina about it," Mariana said. She cocked her head to the side as she watched Len's antics, obviously trying to figure him out.

"Can you describe it?" Len asked. "Did it look like a

liquid, but more viscous?"

"I don't know." Mariana shook her head. "Doc said it was a 'non-Newtonian fluid'."

"I don't know what that means, but I'm—" He circled around as a group of hens closed in on him, clucking happily at their game of tag. "I'm a scientist."

"Then I'm sure you can figure your own way out of a chicken pen." Mariana crossed her arms over her chest and nodded toward the gate.

"Grandpa, please," Sabrina said. "Let me help him."

"Sabrina, he's not who you think he is," grandpa whispered.

Sabrina thought of all the bedtime stories grandpa had told her about Craig and his daring escapades. They were always trying to avoid the evil Coalition.

But things seemed to have changed. Sadirians weren't the bad guys depicted in grandpa's stories. At least, Len wasn't.

"No, grandpa," Sabrina said. "He's not who *you* think he is."

Grandpa looked down at her, his brow furrowed deeply.

"Have I ever brought someone to meet you before?" she said. "Would I have brought him if I didn't think…" She shook her head, not really sure what she thought. She only knew what she felt, and she trusted Len. "You know me better than that."

He let out a sigh, then finally loosened his hold on her.

Sabrina ran over to the chicken pen and started undoing the wire on the gate. By the time she had it open, Len was waiting right on the other side. Sabrina used a foot to shoo the chickens away as he made his escape, then she closed the gate and reattached the wire.

"Thanks for rescuing me," Len said. He was still staring at the chickens. "Seriously, what are those things?"

"Later." Sabrina threaded her arm through Len's elbow, forgetting everything for a moment when he smiled down at her. The moment didn't last long.

"You really should fix that latch, Marvin," Mariana said.

Grandpa grunted. "It works well enough."

"So, you were going to tell me about that chemical," Mariana said.

"I'd have to see it to identify it," Len said. "What did you do with the substance you found?"

"I sent it with Doc to his lab," Mariana said. "He did a real good job gathering it all up—just in case it was dangerous."

"Is it still here in Harbor?" Len asked.

"Yeah." Mariana shrugged. "We don't have a fancy setup, but we get things done."

"I'm sure you do." Len smiled.

"It just looked like liquid Mercury to me," Mariana said. "Which is toxic, and you need permits to have in that kind of quantity."

"Liquid Mercury?" He looked down at Sabrina. "Like

the planet?"

A laugh escaped her before she could stop it. "She's talking about the element. You know, the silvery stuff that looks like a liquid, but kind of sticks to itself. I always thought it seemed kind of alive when we used it in experiments in Chemistry class."

She felt Len's body stiffen next to hers. His smile was still in place when she looked up at him, but it seemed forced—perhaps the first fake expression she'd seen from him.

"Well, then, that's probably what it is," Len said.

"And how'd it get all over the floor in the pet parlor?" Mariana asked.

Len shook his head. "I have no idea."

"And the mangled cage?" she prompted.

"Again..." Len shrugged.

"It's a kennel, not a cage," Sabrina said. "Are the cats okay?" She couldn't believe she hadn't thought to ask yet.

"They were pretty upset when Kimmy found them this morning," Mariana said. "It took a while to round them all up. They'd found lots of hiding places."

"Where are they now?" Sabrina asked. "Mrs. Simpkins's house isn't ready yet."

"Kimmy took them home with her for the night, but they should be back at the parlor now." Mariana shook her head. "I can't imagine living with that many cats."

"It sounds like someone entered the parlor after we left,"

Len said. "I'm just glad we had already gone." He looked at Sabrina, his smile painfully tight. "We really wouldn't have wanted to be there while someone was tearing up the place."

"Says you," Sabrina said. "I wish I *had* been there to fight the creep off."

"I have to agree with your friend," Mariana said. "We're still not even sure what was used on the metal." She gave Len a long, appraising look, then sighed at Sabrina. "You're sure you're all right?"

"I am." Sabrina nodded.

"Okay, then," Mariana said. "I'll head back to Main Street and check in with Doc." She cocked her head at Len. "I'd like you to stay in town for a couple of days. Just in case we need your expertise as a scientist."

Len nodded vigorously. "I have no plans to depart."

"See there?" Sabrina stepped closer to him, daring to wrap her arm around his waist. He looked surprised, but smiled at her as he draped his arm over her shoulders. "Everything's fine."

"Absolutely fine," Len agreed.

Mariana didn't look convinced, but she turned and headed for her SUV. They all just watched her leave, no one daring to speak until the sound of her engine had faded in the distance. The moment it had, Len turned to Sabrina and grasped her arms tightly, his eyes wide with panic.

"Everything is not fine," he said.

Chapter Ten

Quicksilver. The substance the officer described had to be quicksilver. And where there was quicksilver, there were Scorpiians.

"Sabrina, where—" Len's question was cut off as someone grabbed the back of his jacket and nearly lifted him off his feet. He released Sabrina rather than have her be dragged along with him as he was hurled several feet away.

"Grandpa, stop it," Sabrina yelled. "You'll get hurt."

"*He'll* get hurt?" Len barely managed to keep his footing. When he looked over at Marvin to explain, the words stuck in Len's throat.

The Earthling's eyebrows were so low, they had to be obscuring his vision. One side of his face twitched, curling his lip up in a near-snarl. His shoulders were hunched, and his hands tightly fisted at his sides.

The closest thing Len had seen to the man's expression and posture was when Barbara was about to lose her temper. Marvin wasn't as scary as an angry Lyrian, but he was still a formidable presence. Plus, he was Sabrina's grandfather, and after her comment about being "more than friends"," Len really didn't want to upset the man.

"Nobody manhandles my little girl," Marvin said.

"Manhandles?" Len had no idea what that meant. How could a handle be gendered?

"He means he didn't like you grabbing me," Sabrina said, pushing past Marvin.

"I'm sorry, I just—" Len began.

"You were freaking out," she said. "What I don't get is why?"

"It's not our concern." Marvin straightened, but if anything, that just made him more intimidating. He crossed his arms over his broad chest, that same sneer on his face. "I got Craig's message just before Mariana arrived. I know you're from the Coalition."

Even more than Len wanted to try to win over Sabrina's grandpa, he wanted her to be safe. Would it be better if Len used this as an opportunity to handle this on his own? He could always come back and explore her statement later.

He looked over at her, mouth opening and closing as he tried to find the right words. She arched an eyebrow, then crossed her hands over her chest in such a similar pose to Marvin's that Len almost laughed.

No wonder she was protective of her grandpa. The two were so similar.

The look on her face made it clear that if Len tried to leave her behind, it wouldn't end well for him. Besides, he didn't *want* to leave her behind.

They felt like… Like a unit.

Len straightened as he addressed Marvin. "But it should concern you. If you and Craig are as close as I believe you to be, you should know what that silver chemical is."

"Quicksilver." Marvin grunted. "Craig told me you're letting a Scorpiian run around on Earth—which proves you Sadirians are even stupider than I thought."

"Okay, first, I think 'more stupid' is the correct terminology." Len smiled as Sabrina snickered.

Marvin rolled his eyes and murmured, "Lord help me, there's two of them now."

"And second, Zemanni is in Florida," Len said. "He wasn't part of the team sent to collect samples from the cats."

"Cats and scorpions." Sabrina shook her head. "What is with you guys and our animals? Why do you care?"

"He's not talking about the bug, sweetheart," Marvin said. "He's talking about Grays."

Sabrina snorted, but then her brow furrowed. She shifted closer to Len.

"Wait, like…the ones in your stories?" she asked.

"Shapeshifting assassins, bounty-hunters, and low-lifes." Marvin nodded. "If they had hearts, they'd be cold as ice."

Len had seen Zemanni with Brooke, the Earthling who had proven the Scorpiian did indeed have a heart. There was no doubt the two loved each other.

"I think Zemanni's human bondmate would argue that point," Len said.

"What's a bondmate?" Sabrina asked.

"His wife." Marvin grunted again. "And that just shows he's good at duping people. It's what Scorpiians do."

Len let out a laugh. "Forgive me, but if Brooke heard you talking like that, you'd be in for it."

Marvin puffed out his chest, again, reminding Len of a Lyrian. Just how much time had he spent with Craig?

"I'm not afraid of Scorpiians," Marvin said.

"With all due respect, everyone is afraid of Scorpiians," Len said. "Except maybe Brooke. But we have other worries. Zemanni wasn't here. There must be another Scorpiian operating on Earth."

The idea was chilling. Scorpiians were normally very territorial. Even with Zemanni not actively pursuing targets, Len had thought the planet was under some sort of protection from others of his kind just because he'd settled here. Apparently, that was wrong.

"Just how bad are these guys?" Sabrina asked. "I mean, I remember grandpa's stories about them, but surely those were exaggerated."

Marvin shook his head. "Actually, I toned them down for you so you wouldn't have nightmares."

"We need to get to that quicksilver before the Scorpiian does," Len said. "The Earthling who has it is in danger."

"Should you call in reinforcements?" Sabrina asked.

Len shook his head. "We're trying to prevent people from finding out about aliens. The more of us there are in the area, the harder that will be. I know we look human, but our cultural programming sessions aren't perfect."

"No one's going to be asking you about chickens," Sabrina said.

"I'll give you a ride into town," Marvin said, staring pointedly at Len. "And you can take it from there."

"*We* can take it from there." Sabrina crossed her arms and jutted her chin at her grandpa.

"Sabrina, you don't know what you're getting yourself into," Marvin said.

"No, I think you don't." She let out an exasperated sigh. "Grandpa, I've been to his ship. I've been to *outer space.* And now I have a chance to be part of something…"

She looked over at Len and smiled so genuinely, it stole his breath. She grasped his hand and entwined their fingers.

"Something wonderful," she said. When she turned back to Marvin, the steel edge was back in her voice. "And I'm not going to let anyone take that away from me."

Marvin held her stare for a few moments, then looked away and shook his head. "Damn Scorpiian," he murmured. "Doesn't stand a chance."

Sabrina smiled broadly. Marvin dug in one of his pockets and pulled out a set of keys.

"Fine," Marvin said, tossing the keys to Sabrina, who

caught them easily. "Take the truck, but just get the quicksilver and get out. Tell Doc to get to Mariana's, just in case I can't reach him before you do. I'll give your folks a call, too, and let them know you're okay."

"Thank you!" Sabrina started pulling Len along after her as she headed toward a small structure off to the side of the house.

It couldn't be this easy. He couldn't believe Marvin was just letting them go.

"What about you?" Len asked.

Marvin smirked. "I'm going to call in my own reinforcements."

Chapter Eleven

"One thing I don't get about this is, why is a Scorpiian interested in our cats?" Sabrina had been mulling over the question ever since they'd pulled away from grandpa's house. She hadn't been able to come up with any explanation that made a lick of sense.

"I don't know," Len said. "That confused me, too."

"Do you think he'll try to get at them again? I mean, I'm assuming that's why the kennel door was messed up."

"His priority will be to retrieve the quicksilver. That's the substance that enables him to shapeshift. It's worth a fortune on Scorpii-2."

"That's their homeworld?"

"Yes."

She still couldn't believe she was talking about real, live aliens. And *with* a real live alien. A cute one, at that.

And a really good kisser.

"This is Doc's place."

She pulled to the curb and parked the truck, staring out at a street that seemed familiar and unfamiliar at the same time.

Some of the storefronts still had Christmas lights in the windows. She wondered if Len knew what they were. Did they even have holidays where he was from?

She wished it was Spring. If Len was used to space stations and barren dome worlds, he would be floored by the blooming trees all along Main Street, as well as the tulips and hyacinths that would fill all the planters along the road.

Her heart raced at the thought of sharing that with him, feeling an excitement about such a simple thing that she hadn't experienced since she was a child. Nothing would be quite the same for her after this experience with Len.

Her stomach gave a little lurch as she imagined what her life would be like after this adventure. What if Len wasn't part of it? Was he even allowed to get involved with an Earthling?

Marq had a human 'bondmate'. So did Dane. And if a Scorpiian had fallen for someone and was allowed to marry them, then—

She shook her head. This was not something she should be thinking about right now, especially with how recently they'd met. It felt like so much longer though. Life-changing events must do that to a relationship.

She perked up as an older man with thinning white hair walked up to the front windows from inside the shop. He drew down the blinds, but not before she'd seen his big handlebar mustache and wire-framed glasses. That was all the glimpse she needed to know that Doc was in.

"Let's go," she said.

Len fell in step with her on the sidewalk after exiting the truck, their strides matching in a way that made her breath hitch.

How could they be so in sync already? That was a mystery for later. Right now, she needed to stay focused on the quicksilver. As long as he had it, Doc was in danger.

When they reached the door, she rapped on the frosty glass. No one answered.

She pounded more insistently, and yelled, "Doc? It's Sabrina. I know you're there. Open up."

A few more moments passed. She tried the handle, and found it unlocked.

"Come on." She opened the door and stepped inside.

Doc's shop was always a little weird, but today, it was downright creepy. His inventions lined shelves that covered every wall—radios and wires and devices with purposes she couldn't guess at. With the lights off, only the sun that filtered through the closed blinds illuminated the place.

"What function does this human have in your society?" Len asked, looking around at all the odds and ends everywhere.

"He's the local mad scientist, I guess you'd say."

"What's he angry about?"

She stifled a laugh and ended up snorting.

Really attractive, Sabrina.

Len didn't seem to mind, though.

"Not that kind of mad," she said. "Like 'crazy' mad."

"Oh." Len had wandered over to a device with a small satellite-looking dish on it. "Is he an engineer?"

"Of a sort."

Sabrina jumped at the unexpected voice that she totally should have expected. Doc was standing behind a counter that partially blocked the open archway that led deeper into his lab.

"Doc," Sabrina said.

"Sabrina," he parroted back. "Who's your friend?"

"This is Len."

Len smiled and offered his hand to shake. At least he knew that much.

"More than a friend, actually," Len said.

Apparently, he didn't know enough to *not* say that.

"Nice to meet you, Sabrina's more-than-a-friend." Doc reached out and shook Len's hand, holding onto it for what felt like a long time.

Len didn't seem to mind—or maybe he just didn't know any better. Sabrina was kind of surprised he knew about handshakes in the first place, after the whole chicken pen thing.

Finally, Doc released Len's hand and turned to Sabrina. "Now, what can I do for you?"

Crap. They needed a cover story. They couldn't just waltz in and take the quicksilver.

"I'm a scientist," Len said. "We spoke with Sheriff Mariana about the substance you found at the pet parlor and are here to help you out with that."

Wow, that made sense. It was even true, if misleading.

"A scientist, eh?" Doc said. "Well, if Mariana wants you to take a look, I'm not one to argue."

He turned and headed through the archway. Sabrina cast a look at Len, but he simply smiled at her and gestured for her to go first. Her look turned to a glare.

"I'm not getting any younger," Doc called from the other room.

They quickly joined him in what really did look like a mad scientist's lair.

Tubes and beakers and bottles of all sizes and shapes covered every horizontal surface. There were a few upright...science-fridges—Sabrina had no idea what they were called—casting a bluish light that washed out the colors around them. Again, the lights weren't on.

"It's pretty dark back here," Sabrina said. "Are you having trouble with your eyes, Doc?"

"A bit."

As Doc turned around, Len gasped and reached for Sabrina, but stopped as suddenly as he'd started to move. He looked like he'd been frozen in place, arms outstretched toward her. She almost expected a sheet of ice to form around him.

"Len?" She took a step closer, but Doc let out a tutting

noise.

"I wouldn't do that if I were you." Doc blinked at her—his eyelids closing sideways. *Sideways.*

His eyes were completely black, even the parts that should be white. Just like the Grays in grandpa's stories.

Panic chewed at the edges of her thought. She pushed it away with the best tool she had—anger.

"What did you do to Len?" she demanded.

Not-Doc waved a small silver disk at her.

"Stasis disk," he said. "It's a primitive Sadirian technology, but it gets the job done. Unfortunately, the field isn't very refined. You'll sting your fingers if you get too close to your 'more-than-a-friend'."

"Is he okay?"

"He's fine. That's why they call it a 'stasis disk' and not a 'damage disk' or something equally ridiculous. Sadirians love dramatic names, but they aren't very creative."

"What about Doc?" She wasn't sure she wanted to know, but at the same time had to. "What did you do to him?"

"He's unharmed. For now. I'm keeping him in a much more civilized stasis chamber on my ship."

Sabrina didn't like how forthcoming this guy was with information. Wasn't that a sign that he was going to kill her? But he hadn't made any threatening moves. Toward her, at least.

"I'm assuming you have your quicksilver already,"

Sabrina said. "Why don't you just leave?"

Not-Doc chuckled. "Because that's not all I want. And you're going to help me."

"I don't think so."

"You're a fearless little creature, aren't you?"

It felt like a rhetorical question, so she amped up her glare.

The entire situation was surreal. She felt like she was stuck in a B sci-fi movie. If she let go of her attitude, she feared her grasp on reality would suffer permanent consequences.

As if on cue, his face suddenly morphed, eyes becoming enormous and his skin a pasty gray. Lines of scratches criss-crossed his features, especially around his eyes. The skin around the scratches was puffy and swollen, a slightly darker shade from the rest.

Mrs. Simpkins's cats had really done a number on him. It helped Sabrina swallow down the remainder of her panic.

He rested his fingers against the marks, gingerly pressing them back into place until he looked like Doc again.

"I guess I'm not the only 'fearless little creature' you've encountered on Earth," she said.

He smiled at her, the sight unnerving. "You'll learn."

Chapter Twelve

Len had never been aboard a Scorpiian vessel. His curiosity was hardly satisfied by watching plain ceiling panels passing above him as he floated through the corridors in an anti-grav field. His heart raced, trapped in a body that couldn't move otherwise.

They finally came to a stop in what looked like a small room. He could see Sabrina standing next to him. Ever defiant, she was staring down the Scorpiian.

"Aren't you going to let him go?" she asked.

Gravity reasserted itself at the same time the stasis field dropped—along with Len. Sabrina gasped, reaching out to try to catch him. It was a futile but touching gesture. She ended up toppled across his chest.

The door hissed shut, leaving them sealed in a small, empty chamber.

"That's not what I meant, you jerk," Sabrina yelled.

"I doubt he can hear you." Len looked around, hoping for an access panel, a comm relay, even a bit of furniture to make the place more comfortable. Okay, and maybe use as a weapon.

There was nothing.

He couldn't kid himself. There was no chance of escape. He couldn't even hope that Marvin would be able to get them help.

Scorpiian vessels were as undetectable as Lyrian ships. Even if Craig or soldiers from the Coalition came to Doc's shop looking for them, they wouldn't be able to find them.

Len rested his head on the floor. Sabrina was still half-lying across his chest. That was by far the most pleasant part of his current situation.

"Are you okay?" she said.

There was no sense scaring her. And yet, he knew she would want the truth.

She ran her fingers across his cheek, then reached to feel the back of his head. He closed his eyes, enjoying the feel of her touch against his scalp.

"Len..."

Her breath was warm against his face. If he asked, maybe she would let him kiss him again. He'd like to do that once more before they met their fate.

No. Dammit, no. He had to stop thinking like this. He had to find a way to save her.

"I'm fine," he said.

"Then why are you lying on the floor?"

"I'm enjoying the attention."

She snorted. "There will be time for that later. Right now, we have to figure a way out of here."

"Sabrina—" He opened his eyes, but the words caught in his throat when he looked up at her.

Her eyes were so bright. Her hair caught the dim light in the room and seemed to glow. And even in this desperate situation, he could barely see a hint of fear in her face. He sat up and cupped her cheek in one hand, hoping to ease even that trace of the unwelcome emotion.

"The Scorpiian wants something from you," Len said. "You can use that to get through this."

"I'm not helping him, whatever it is he wants."

"If it keeps you alive, you will."

That glare of hers hit him full-force. This time, he only laughed. He didn't even move his hand away.

"When the Scorpiian returns, I'll distract him," Len said. "You saw the path he took to get here. You can retrace your steps and escape."

Her mouth fell open. "I'm not leaving without you."

Len shook his head. "I have no value to him. I'm actually not sure why the Scorpiian hasn't disintegrated me yet."

"Don't say that." Her face paled.

"I'm sorry, but it's the truth. And I've always tried to give you the truth. I won't stop now."

"Len…" Her eyes glittered. The sight felt like a black hole opening in his chest.

"Stop being stupid," she said. "We're getting out of this together."

Len laughed. "I know too much to share your optimism in this case," he said. "But you... You can get through this. You are one of the strongest people I've ever met."

She tried to look away, but he held her tight.

"I mean it." He dusted a few locks of hair back behind her ear. "And I've met sentients from hundreds of systems. No one has ever affected me the way you do."

"That's quite a line," she said.

"A line?"

She sighed and glanced away. Her cheeks turned a little pink.

"Something you say to try to get a person to...you know," she said.

"I don't know."

She held his gaze for a few moments then said, "You really don't, do you? I mean, your people... You have sex, right?"

He felt his eyebrows hitch up. He had to clear his throat before he could respond.

"Yes," he said. "I mean, some people do. Most of us just use *Coupling*, though."

"Now I'm the one who's confused."

"*Coupling* is a drug that the High Council encouraged citizens to use. It takes the body through all the stages of arousal and culmination."

"That sounds so...boring." She let out a little laugh, but then her brow furrowed. "Wait, you said, 'most of *us*'.

Have you only ever used *Coupling?*"

He shrugged. "I believe the Earth phrase is, 'I don't get out much'."

He chuckled, but she didn't join him. Her lips set in a line.

And then she dove forward and kissed him.

He barely was able to keep his balance. Her lips crushed against his, passion and desperation pulling at him to give in and be swept along with her. But they were in a holding cell on a Scorpiian vessel. He gripped her arms to still her and managed to lean away.

"Sabrina, what are you doing?"

"Making sure I don't have any regrets."

She pulled her coat off and threw it on the floor behind him, then pushed him back on it. This time, he didn't resist her kiss.

Her warm lips moved against his, her tongue stroking the seam of his mouth. He let her in, molten pleasure flooding his system at the taste of her.

His hands settled on her hips as she straddled him, the soft fabric of her pajamas muting the contact. He wanted more, and she seemed to as well.

He ran his hands up under the bulky material of her top. She let out a gasp as his hands brushed against her skin. He used the opportunity to deepen the kiss, flattening his hands against her back and pressing her closer to him. He rolled them over, nestling himself between her legs and letting out a groan as he felt her heat even through their clothing.

His dick was so hard. No chemicals. No *Coupling*. It was just him and Sabrina and nothing had ever felt so good.

She tugged at his jacket, and he leaned back long enough to tear it off and throw it aside. While he did, she pulled his shirt free from his pants. She slid her hands up along his stomach, lighting up his nerves like a solar storm.

"Off," she ordered, tugging at his shirt.

He helped her get it over his head and added it to the pile on the floor around them.

"Damn, Len," she said, staring at his chest. "You act like a geek, but you look like *this* under your clothes?"

He glanced down at his chest, unsure what she meant. "Like what?"

"Like a supermodel." She raked her fingertips down his chest and shook her head. "I only wish we had more time. When do you think the Scorpiian will come back?"

"I'm not sure. He's probably regenerating, so we have a little time."

"Then we should hurry."

She grabbed the fastener for his pants and undid it, rising up on her knees to kiss him again. She slid her hand past the waistband of his undergarment and gripped his dick.

Sensation exploded through him again, pulses of pleasure beating along his nerves. She squeezed his shaft harder, running her hand up and down along its length.

This wasn't a solar storm. It was a quasar. The room was spinning, his heartbeat thundering in his ears. He could feel himself building to an event horizon, and didn't know what was on the other side.

But he knew *who* was on the other side. Sabrina. And as long as she was with him, the impossible seemed possible.

"I wish we had more time." Her words were a breathless whisper against his ear.

"Who knows," he said. "Maybe we can get through this after all."

She pulled away from him and rose to her feet. At first, disappointment battled with the lust clouding his mind. But then she unbuttoned her shirt and let it fall to the ground. Her pajama bottoms quickly followed, as well as her boots and socks, leaving her naked before him.

"You want more of this, you better be ready to fight for it," she said.

He stood and closed the distance between them. Burying one hand in her hair, he pulled her up against him and said, "I will be."

Chapter Thirteen

This was so unlike any of her fantasies about being abducted and taken aboard an alien vessel. But the moment Len kissed her again, she knew she wouldn't change a thing.

His hands explored her body, eager and yet hesitant. She couldn't believe he'd never been with someone before. The guy was a natural. If only they had more time to truly learn each other's bodies.

She would be grateful for what they had. She would hold onto it. And dammit, they were going to fight their way out of this—together.

She slid a hand between them, reaching for his dick again and hoping her body would be able to handle him. For all that he acted and talked like her dream nerd, he looked like a professional swimmer, all lean lines and muscle.

He hissed in a breath as she worked him, his hips moving against her hand.

Definitely good instincts in this one.

He reached down to grab her thigh, lifting it to hook

over his hip. Then he slid his hand back along it, not stopping when he reached her slit.

Fantastic instincts.

He worked through her slick folds, spreading her. He slid one finger into her core, then another.

She moaned against his mouth, squeezed his dick harder. Sparks were starting to go off behind her eyelids.

"Len," she said. "I need you. Now."

Thank God he understood what she meant this time. He lowered them to the floor again, laying her on the pile of their discarded clothes. After pushing down his pants and boxer-briefs, he lined himself up with her core.

"Sabrina..." he murmured against her ear. He buried his face in the nape of her neck.

Slowly, he pushed forward, parting her sex. She felt herself stretching for him, gripping him tight. He kept on that steady pressure until he'd buried himself as deep as he could, his hips grinding against her clit.

His body trembled and his eyes were pinched shut. Sabrina barely dared to blink. She didn't want to miss a moment of this.

Just as slowly, he pulled back, sucking in a hissing breath between his teeth.

"Nothing can feel this good," he said.

She grabbed the back of his head, angling him so she could kiss him again. He thrust his tongue into her mouth, sparring with her, savoring her, taking everything she had to give.

His hips started to move faster, his strokes more urgent. Her nerves felt electrified, sensation coursing through her. She clenched her core around his shaft as tight as she could, trying to pull everything out of this blissful encounter that she could.

The pressure built, more sparks shining against her eyelids. Len paused for a brief moment, then let out a guttural moan and began pounding into her.

The sparks turned into a firework show that lit up her entire body. She felt him pulsing deep inside her, her body beating back its own cadence in return. When she felt that she might black out from the pleasure, it finally abated.

Len was buried as deep in her as he could be, his arms clenched around her. She was holding onto him just as tight.

She wouldn't let go of him. Wouldn't give up. They would get through this somehow. She just had to make sure he believed that, too.

"As amazing as that was," she managed through gasping breaths, "it can be even better."

Len cast an incredulous look at her.

"I'll prove it to you," she said. "All you have to do is survive."

She pushed on his shoulder, and he rolled off of her, but not far away. She liked that he didn't seem to want to leave her side. At the same time, she didn't want to be naked when that Scorpiian returned.

Grabbing her clothes as she stood, she took a moment to enjoy seeing Len stretched out below her. His lean body made her drool. There were so many things she wanted to do with him, so many things to explore—and not just in bed, when they finally made it to one.

She knew she could be abrasive. Len seemed to not only get that about her but to actually enjoy her personality. He accepted and appreciated her just as she was. And he was sweet and smart and…fun, their current circumstances notwithstanding.

"Get dressed," she said, pulling her pajama top on and starting to button it up. "We need to be ready when that jackass returns."

Len rose to his feet. He seemed a little wobbly, which made her smile. *She* had done that to him. It was hard for her to believe that was his first time.

By the time she was dressed, Len was, too. They were pulling on their coats just as the door whooshed open.

Sabrina crossed her arms and amped up her glare to be as baleful as she could manage.

"Look what *the cat* dragged in," she said.

Not-Doc paused in the doorway. His eyes looked normal now. Len was probably right about him regenerating.

"I don't know what a cat is," the Scorpiian said. "But I assure you nothing drags me anywhere."

He didn't know what a cat was? She guessed that made

sense, after Len's confusion about chickens.

"Well, nobody drags me anywhere, too," she said. "So if you want something from me, you better start talking."

Not-Doc cocked his head to the side. "You're a curious Earthling. Most of the ones I've encountered aren't so…"

"Confident?" she said. "Take-charge?"

He smiled. "Arrogant."

Len stepped closer to her and murmured, "Coming from a Scorpiian, that's actually kind of a compliment."

"I don't want compliments," she said. "I want to leave."

"Fair enough." Not-Doc stepped away from the door and gestured toward the hall.

There was no way this could be that easy. Sabrina looked to Len, who seemed equally skeptical. She reached out and took his hand before moving toward the door.

Not-Doc smirked. "As I thought. You've achieved a pair-bond."

Len balked, quickly dropping her hand. "That's just an Earth mannerism."

"I believe I've studied Earth mannerisms more than you have," Not-Doc said. "And it's obvious you both care for each other."

Why was it a bad thing for the Scorpiian to know about that? Len had gone pale and would only cast the quickest of looks her way.

"Lucky me," Not-Doc said. "Now, you're going to help me, Earthling, or your Sadirian bondmate will pay the price."

Oh. Yeah, that definitely made it a bad thing.

"Why don't you just tell me what you want, already?" Sabrina said.

The Scorpiian's smirk deepened. She wished the cats had scratched his mouth right off his face.

"Those animals you're keeping in your prison," he said. "What are they?"

"Prison?" Sabrina racked her brain for what he meant. Only one thing made the slightest sense. "Do you mean our pet parlor?"

Not-Doc paused. "A parlor implies a place of comfort, not one with bars sealing holding cells."

Righteous indignation joined in with her baseline anger, pushing any remaining fear completely aside.

"We keep our guests very comfortable," she said. "And we're working toward improving our facilities."

"Guests. Hmm." He nodded thoughtfully. "What makes these 'guests' so special that a Vegan is interested in them?"

How the heck did this guy know about Cyan?

"Are they potential weapons?" he asked. With a straight face.

Sabrina stifled the urge to laugh. She glanced over at Len. He looked as serious as Not-Doc. They really knew next to nothing about cats.

I can use that.

"Quid pro quo," she said. Not-Doc cocked his head to

the side. "It means, you do something for me and I do something for you. Starting with you releasing Doc."

"First, answer a question," he said. "The injuries I received in their attack injected some sort of toxins into my system that were challenging to remove."

Sabrina had heard of "cat scratch fever" and knew that cat scratches and bites could become infected pretty easily. She also remembered how *War of the Worlds* had ended.

This guy was still standing, so apparently cat germs weren't enough to take him out, but it still gave her hope. She could find a way to use this.

"Are those creatures meant to be used as bioweapons?" Not-Doc said.

"Yes." She couldn't believe she managed to sound so convincing. She could feel manic giggles building up in her chest. "Now free Doc."

The Scorpiian took one step backward and the door to their room whooshed shut again. The moment it did, Len's composure faltered.

"Oh my God," he said. "Those things are bioweapons? And you keep them as *pets*? They've been running around on our ship. I've *played* with them before."

"Relax." Sabrina looked around the room, uncertain if they were being monitored. "Are you sure he's not watching us or listening in?"

She'd been so caught up in the moment before, that hadn't even occurred to her.

"Scorpiians are arrogant," he said. "Just wait till you meet Zemanni."

She still didn't feel safe. What a perfect excuse to get closer to Len again.

She closed the distance between them and wrapped her arms around his neck, pulling him close. His hands slid around her almost like a reflex.

Whispering in his ear as low as she could, she said, "He asked me to answer questions, not tell the truth."

Len stiffened. "If he finds out..."

"We'll be in just as much trouble as before. I think I have an idea that might get us out of this." She leaned back to look in his eyes and said, "Can you trust me?"

"Absolutely."

No hesitation. No little twitches giving away that he had doubts. He really did believe in her.

She was determined to live up to his trust.

Chapter Fourteen

The Scorpiian was gone for longer than Len expected. At one point, he even feared he felt the ship vibrating, as if it was moving. He hoped that was just nerves. Otherwise, how could anyone ever find them?

The door slid open, and a tall man with unruly brown hair walked in. He was dressed in a type of Earth uniform Len hadn't seen, dark jacket and pants with a deep blue shirt, and a matching thin strip of fabric tied around his neck—all in a sleek fabric that caught the light. The effect was oddly imposing.

"I hope you don't mind that I changed into someone more comfortable," he said. "Dean is one of my favorite forms."

Sabrina shifted closer to Len, earning a smirk from "Dean".

"Where is Doc?" she asked.

"Safely at home in his bed," Dean said. "He'll wake up a little groggy, but will be fine otherwise."

"And I'm supposed to just believe you?"

Her question struck Len as a little ironic, given that she

was intentionally misleading the Scorpiian. Len hoped his expression didn't give anything away.

"We can stop by his house to check, if you'd like," Dean said. "*After* we visit your 'pet parlor'."

"Why do you want to go back there?" Sabrina asked.

"For the bioweapons." He stepped away from the door and once again gestured for them to exit the room.

This time, Sabrina took him up on the offer. Len followed her into the hallway.

Seeing the inside of a Scorpiian vessel actually dulled his fear at their situation. Instead of command panels etched into the walls, there were occasional rectangles that shimmered and rippled, like a thin layer of quicksilver was held on its surface. Len leaned closer to one, trying to get a better look.

"Keep moving," Dean said.

Sabrina reached out for Len's hand, walking a bit awkwardly in the narrow hallway. The corridors were even more nondescript than the Coalition vessels and space stations Len was used to. He infinitely preferred the lush greenery, open spaces, and scenic views within Vegan ships.

After a few turns and passing through a small chamber, they reached an exit hatch. Dean stood next to one of the quicksilver control panels.

"Don't try anything foolish," he said. "I don't need a weapon to kill you."

He lifted his left arm, wiggling his fingers. As they watched, the fingers fused together, his skin turning gray, then silver. His entire forearm sharpened to a gleaming point. He stabbed it into the control panel.

The quicksilver of his ship rippled and pulsed. Dean let out a breath, then removed his arm from the wall. By the time it was back at his side, it looked completely normal.

The hatch opened, letting in a chill breeze. Sabrina cast a last look at Len, then stepped out into the empty lot at the back of the pet parlor.

Dusk arrived early during this time of the year and in this section of the planet. The sun was already setting, making the temperature drop. Len was grateful for the jacket Sabrina had given him.

At the back door, Sabrina reached into her pocket and pulled out a set of keys.

"Careful," Dean said, forming his arm into a sharp point again and bringing it to rest on Len's back. "I don't need him alive to gather my targets."

Sabrina turned with the keys between her fingers, each sticking out as their own sharp point. "If you hurt him, I swear to God, I'll make you pay."

Len appreciated the gesture, but knew she'd never stand a chance against a Scorpiian. Dean merely smirked. He nodded toward the door.

Sabrina turned back to unlock it, then led them inside.

The door to the kennel area stood open. As they

approached, Len could see that the mess they'd left earlier had been cleaned up.

The door of the kennel that had originally held the cats had been removed, but the cats themselves were sleeping in another just next to it. One lifted its head to look in their direction, then immediately leapt up and started making an awful noise.

The hair on its body stood on end, making it look twice as big as before. It arched its back, revealing rows of menacing teeth. Len had never seen anything like it. The other cats quickly woke and did the same, all staring balefully at the Scorpiian and yowling.

Dean actually jerked back, lifting his spike-arm defensively.

"Relax," Sabrina said. "I know how to handle them."

"What are they?" A tinge of wonder colored Dean's voice. "The way they seem to alter their size and appearance... It's almost as if they can change their shape."

"They're called cats," she said. "We Earthlings keep them as pets."

Dean's eyebrows hiked up his forehead, a strangely genuine reaction in a being infamous for hiding its true nature. "I don't know whether that's impressive or insane," he said.

A sharp voice entered the conversation. "What's insane is my best friend not calling me after whatever the hell went down in our pet parlor last night!"

"Kimmy…" Sabrina paled as another Earthling entered the room. She was a little shorter than Sabrina, and had long dark hair—the same color as her glasses and clothing.

Dean quickly lowered his arm, but Len could see the glint of silver on it still.

"Why didn't you call me?" Kimmy pulled Sabrina into a hug so tight, Len's bones creaked in sympathy. "When I met Mariana here, I totally freaked out."

"I left my phone…somewhere," Sabrina said.

"Oh right." Kimmy reached into a pocket and pulled out a phone covered in pictures of dogs.

"Thank you." Sabrina took the phone and slipped it into her own pocket. "Where are Pancakes and Fluffy?"

"Oh, they were picked up earlier this morning," Kimmy said. "Trevor heard about the shenanigans and wanted them home. It took me a couple of hours to calm down Mrs. Simpkins and convince her her babies were safer here than in her house, with the paint still off-gassing. If her house was ready, she'd have taken them, too. This isn't going to be good for our business."

"We'll be fine," Sabrina said.

"I know, I just like to worry." Kimmy threaded her elbow through Sabrina's arm and leaned against her, turning toward Dean and Len. "So anyway, who are your friends? And which one is for me?"

"I'm Len." Len took the opportunity to move closer to Sabrina and farther from the Scorpiian. Dean didn't look happy about it, but he didn't move to stop him.

"And I'm more than a friend," Len said.

"Ooo." Kimmy smiled at him, then shook his hand. "Then I'm very glad to meet you, indeed. And I somewhat understand why my very best friend in the whole world didn't call me when she knew I would be terribly worried about her."

"I've been keeping her busy," Len said.

Kimmy's eyebrows rose at that. "I bet you have." She turned to Dean and said, "And who are you, then?"

"Friend of Len's," Dean said. "Just a friend."

"Glad to hear it." Kimmy's voice had taken on a breathy quality. She started toward Dean, but Sabrina tightened her grip on Kimmy's arm.

"I'm really sorry I worried you," Sabrina said. "Let me make it up to you by closing tonight. Len can help me. And Dean." She scowled at Dean when she said his name.

"It's fine," Kimmy said. "I totally get it. It's about freaking time you found somebody who appreciates you. Now we just need to find someone for me to hook up with."

Kimmy's gaze went up and down Dean's frame. Was she interested in starting a relationship with Dean? Len suppressed a shiver.

"Why don't we all go out and grab a bite to eat?" Kimmy said. "Cheryl's diner has killer pie."

"Killer, eh?" Dean said. "That sounds interesting."

"You know what?" Sabrina's voice had risen in pitch. "Why don't you go ahead and get us a table?"

"Sabrina." Kimmy managed to extricate herself from Sabrina's hold. "What's going on with you? Are you trying to get rid of me?"

"I believe she is." Dean pulled the stasis disk from his pocket. "And I am not okay with that."

Len lunged for the disk, but before he could take two steps, Dean had modified his arm again. Len barely managed to stop before impaling himself on the sharp point. Sabrina ran to his side, pulling him back.

"What the hell?" Kimmy said.

Dean pointed the stasis disk at her and activated it.

"If we're done with the 'diversions' section of this interaction, could we please move on to the actual objective?" Dean said. "I now control the fate of two people you care about. Give me the bioweapons."

"I will," Sabrina said. "Just... You saw for yourself how dangerous they can be. And you have them all riled up. I have to calm them down first."

Dean nodded. "Proceed."

Sabrina cast a look at Len that he didn't quite understand. Her eyes were pinched, her brow furrowed in worry. But the intensity of her gaze let him know that she was trying to communicate with him. He didn't know what about until she walked over to a counter that ran along the wall and picked up her stun-gun.

"This is a device we use to calm them," she said.

Dean cocked his head to the side. "That looks like a weapon. Primitive, but still."

"It's not," she said. "Let me show you."

"On him." Dean nodded toward Len.

"Wait a minute." Len didn't want to be shot with that device. Especially without Cyan around to nullify the electrifying effect.

"Of course," Sabrina said.

"What?" Len turned toward her, and again was met with that intense stare.

"I didn't get a chance to fully demonstrate this before," she said. "But it can have a calming effect."

She had told him it would electrocute him. How was that calming?

"Trust me," she said.

He swallowed hard, but nodded. This had to be part of her plan.

She pulled the trigger. The two needles shot across the room and lodged in his chest again. He winced, waiting for the rest.

"Isn't that nice?" Sabrina said. "Soothing?"

What the...

She'd only fired the darts. Suddenly her plan made sense. Len forced himself to relax, lowering his shoulders and letting out a deep breath.

"You're right," he said. "That is calming."

"See?" Sabrina walked back to Len and pulled out the needles, then reset the stun-gun. "I just have to use this on the cats, and they'll calm right down."

Okay, maybe her plan didn't make sense.

Sabrina turned to Dean and said, "But you should stand near them while I do. That way, they'll associate you with the positive stimulus."

Okay, now it makes sense again.

Dean still looked wary—both of Sabrina and the cats—but he moved to stand where she indicated. Sabrina started talking to the cats, making soft cooing noises. They had stopped their own racket when Kimmy entered the room, but still had their backs arched and fur fluffed out as they stared at Dean.

"It's okay," Sabrina said. "Dean is your new friend. Now let me just…"

She fiddled with the stun-gun, as if she was having trouble with it, then pointed it toward the cage. "Here we go."

At the last second, she jerked her hand toward Dean, firing the needles at him instead. His eyes widened for a moment, but then she activated the electric charge.

Dean's body began to shake. His skin cycled between shades from green to purple before settling on gray. His form changed along with each color, features morphing into the faces of dozens of other sentients.

Len didn't know he could feel sorry for a Scorpiian.

Sabrina didn't let up, even when Dean fell to the ground, reverting to his true form.

His head looked overlarge for his thin neck. Spindly limbs spread at strange angles where he fell, and he stared up at them blankly from huge black eyes.

Len took a risk and kicked Dean's hand with his booted foot, knocking the stasis disk loose. Kimmy fell as she was released, but Len caught her.

"What the hell is happening?" Kimmy yelled.

"Aliens are real and this one is an asshole!" Sabrina's device finally ran out of power, judging by the disgusted grunt she let out when the charge stopped. She threw it at Dean's prone body.

"Don't you ever threaten the people I love again!" she yelled. She started toward Dean, but Len grabbed her and pulled her back. He wasn't sure who he was protecting at that point.

"Maybe we should put some distance between us and him before he recovers?" Len said.

Dean was already starting to stir. Sabrina noticed. She looked around the room frantically.

Len knew that look. He'd been on the receiving end of her temper. She was looking for a weapon.

Nothing they had in the room would work against a Scorpiian. Except maybe…

Len grabbed the latch to the cage holding the cats. It was much simpler than the wire wrapped around and around the gate to the chicken enclosure. In seconds, he had the door unlocked and open. He leapt aside as the first cat flung itself out of the opening.

As Len had hoped, the cat went straight for Dean, just as the Scorpiian managed to get to his feet. Two of the others followed in the attack. They hit the ground and immediately bounced up, latching onto Dean with their claws and biting at him.

The attack was brutal. Dean let out a shrill, piercing shriek. His skin rippled, turning a duller shade of gray as it seemed to harden. Len wasn't sure if it was a defense mechanism or a reaction to the injuries that cats were inflicting.

The cats clawed at him, still trying to find purchase. Dean managed to smack them off of him, then ran out of the room. Len leapt forward and slammed the door shut before the cats could follow.

"Oh my God." Kimmy had grabbed onto Sabrina and was clinging to her tight, eyes wide. "Aliens are real."

Chapter Fifteen

An hour later, Sabrina was handing Kimmy a warm cup of tea at grandpa's house. The cats were lounging on various furniture or laps—including Craig's. One of the nestling's tentacles was sticking out of Craig's pouch and gently petting Sleepy, the gray kitten sprawled on the back of his chair.

"I still can't believe you showed up right after that Scorpiian ran off," Sabrina said.

"Well, I had to track you down," Craig said. "And *I* still can't believe that you ran off a Scorpiian using these darling little creatures."

"If you'd been ten minutes earlier you could have…" Sabrina shrugged. "I don't know, arrested him or something."

"There isn't a prison that can hold a Scorpiian," Len said.

Craig rolled his eyes. "Maybe in the Coalition. Anyway, it sounds like you handled things fine on your own."

Kimmy stared at Craig, her tea teetering in her hands. Sabrina righted it, then sat on the couch between Kimmy and Len.

"I still can't believe aliens are real," Kimmy said. "I mean, I'm looking right at him, and I still can't believe it."

"You get used to it, sweetie," Craig said.

Kimmy shook her head. "It's not just that." She turned to Sabrina and said, "You've been so against believing in aliens, and here they are in your grandpa's living room. I mean, you're *dating* one."

Sabrina felt her cheeks heat. But yeah, she supposed she was.

She reached out to hold Len's hand, interlacing their fingers and bringing his hand to rest on her lap. She wasn't sure how long they would have together, but she did know she would fight like crazy to never let him go.

Kimmy went on, as she usually did. "Meanwhile, I've been hoping that my paranormal romances are actually documentaries, and I get nothing. Craig is real. Spaceships are real. Grays are real. Is it too much to ask to run into a vampire?"

Len leaned forward so he could look at Kimmy past Sabrina. "Actually, Brendan, the Earthling who founded the Department of Homeworld Security, calls the Tau Ceti 'vampire space frogs'," Len said. "And there are two Tau Ceti on our team. I could introduce you."

Sabrina liked the sound of that. She wanted to be more involved in his life.

"Oh, cool," Kimmy said. "Wait, did you say vampire

space *frogs*?"

"Yes." Len looked confused.

"Frogs," Kimmy repeated.

Len nodded, finally picking up on her issue. "They look human, though. Except that Kyle is green."

Kimmy shook her head, then turned to grandpa. "You were right all along. I'm sorry I didn't believe you."

Grandpa laughed. "Don't worry about it."

"I'm sorry, too," Sabrina said. Her cheeks stung and her eyes started to fill with tears.

"Hey, it's okay." Grandpa reached across the space between them to pat her knee. He glared at Len before leaning back in his chair, and Len shifted uneasily next to her.

"How are we supposed to keep this secret?" Sabrina said. "I mean, I've spent my whole life telling people you were wrong, and to just leave you alone, but now I know and—"

"Don't worry about it," grandpa said, with more force. "If I'd had more sense and wasn't drunk as a skunk the first time I met Craig, I wouldn't have said anything about it myself. And I shouldn't have kept on about it after. As soon as I saw the effect it was having on you at school, I stopped, but the cat was out of the bag by then."

Len leaned closer and whispered, "Why was the cat in the bag in the first place?"

Sabrina whispered back. "I'll explain later."

"Actually, when I returned to the *Reckoning*, I met with several of our key leaders," Craig said. "Antareans, Vegans, Sadirians, and Earthlings."

Grandpa lifted his arms for a moment to make room for Grumpy, the fluffy white Persian, to jump onto his lap. "About what?"

"Well, we've been looking for a place for visiting aliens to be able to see what life on Earth is life," Craig said. "We also need a group of Earthlings to start adapting to Coalition and Vegan technology, just to see how it goes."

"Like a test group," Len said.

Craig nodded. "Exactly."

"And you want Harbor to be that test group?" Sabrina felt her excitement rise.

They would need help setting it up. Len's people would need to send representatives. He could be one of them. And she would be able to talk to people about her grandpa being right. Everyone would know.

"It would take a lot to make that happen," grandpa said. "And we would all still have to keep aliens a secret from the rest of the world. The whole damned town."

"But wouldn't it be worth it?" Sabrina asked him.

Grandpa made the half-growl, half-grunt sound that let her know he knew she had a point, then looked away.

"That Scorpiian is still out there," Craig said. "And once they have their minds set on something they think has value, they don't shift it. These cats might be able to take care of themselves, but Harbor is going to need protection."

"What do you think?" She turned to Len, hoping that he was as excited as she was, that he wanted to continue whatever this was that they'd found. "Can we do this? Is it possible?"

"As long as Harbor can keep our secret..." He smiled and said, "I'll make some calls."

Epilogue

Serac was grateful the hangar bay was far from command. He needed to think, he needed to plan.

He needed to get this over with.

At least his scout vessel was already prepped for departure, just in case his meeting with the captain didn't go well. Living aboard the small craft he'd stolen had many benefits.

'You fear being exiled again.'

He paused with his hands around the first rung of the ladder that led to the uppermost deck. Frost spread out from his grip and his breath came out as a fog, his *zyln*—the elemental spirit within him—making itself known.

'And you don't?' Serac thought.

His *zyln* was quiet for a moment before responding. *'Some things are worth the risk.'*

And that was at the crux of it. His *zyln* sensed something in this mission. A possibility that neither of them understood, but that Serac was driven to explore.

He began his climb, thinking through what he needed to tell the captain and how best to explain in a way that wouldn't set either of them off. A fight between a Centauran and a Lyrian—even one only a few centuries old, like their captain—could destroy the ship, and not all of their crewmates were so sturdy.

Serac would be forthright and speak plainly. He would restate his loyalty to his captain and crew and that he had chosen—and still chose—to leave his old life behind.

He walked along the curving hallway that circled the bridge, but paused just outside the open doorway that led to the space, collecting himself.

"Serac, I smelled your wariness from three levels down." The captain's booming voice echoed out from command. "Enter and speak, or go back to your ship and take a shower."

Serac took a deep breath, then strode into the room. He ignored the curious stares of the blue-skinned Cygnian at her security station and the oversized Tau Ceti using his cybernetics to dock with the ship's navigation systems.

Serac dropped to one knee and bowed in front of his captain.

"Oh, this will be good," the captain said. "What's brought on this full display of Centauran hierarchy?"

"Captain," Serac began.

"Hank."

Serac's hackles rose at the familiar name the captain insisted his crew use with him. And such an odd name, at that. One from the same obscure planet that was frontmost on Serac's mind.

"Hank," Serac said. "I've been contacted by an old colleague of mine. One who doesn't yet know that we have altered our mission objectives."

"And?" Hank prompted.

"He believes he has found something that is of incalculable worth."

"And?" Hank repeated.

Serac's hackles rose further. The hairs on his arms elongated as his muscles rippled beneath his skin.

He closed his eyes and took a deep breath, then let it out slowly. A puff of icy vapor escaped his chest.

Hank waved the cloud away with one of his four hands. "Elders' feet, out with it."

"He wishes me to join him in securing the prize."

"Hmm." Hank leaned back in his chair, three hands gripping the armrests of the enormous seat while the fourth scratched his chin. "He knows you're part of my crew."

"He does."

"And he believes this prize is worth risking my wrath," Hank said. "Or did he think you wouldn't tell me?"

"Perhaps both. He... He's Scorpiian."

Nadiira straightened from her console, staring at Serac openly. Even Dregal pivoted his chair to watch.

"A Scorpiian." Hank leaned so far forward in his chair that the two hands holding his armrests were all that kept him from falling forward. The other two were left alarmingly available.

Hank was huge, even by Lyrian standards. Eight feet and four hundred pounds of white fur, muscle, and arms capable of ripping things—and sentients—to shreds. He smiled, revealing rows of sharp teeth.

"A Scorpiian," he repeated. "You never told me you had such 'colleagues' in your past."

"With respect," Serac said, "you never asked."

Hank snorted out a hot breath of air, the vapors visible in the cold that Serac couldn't keep himself from emitting. Whatever his *zyln* sensed in their future, it had them both on edge.

A deep rumble started in Hank's chest. The sound rolled out, building into laughter that vibrated through the floor beneath Serac's knee.

Leaning back, Hank shook his head.

"Just when I thought you couldn't surprise me," he said.

"I haven't responded," Serac said. "I know our new objective is important."

"We've only begun taking over Craig and Barbara's operations." Hank snorted again, frowning deeply. "Since they have chosen to shirk their duties to their fellow sentients and leave the work of replenishing stripped worlds to us."

"There's more," Serac said.

Hank waved a hand at him. "Do go on."

"The prize is located on Earth."

"Earth?" Hank said. "Earth."

Serac knew enough to keep his silence. Hank brooded for a few moments, then his eyes widened and a smile spread across his face.

"Once again, you have brought me a great opportunity," Hank said. "Better than you know. You will investigate this lead."

"Captain?"

The fact that Hank didn't correct him worried Serac even more. What did the crafty Lyrian have in mind?

"As our scout, it's your duty to find us new sources," Hank said. "Earth is a planet with preservation status. With the Coalition busy fighting their war and Craig and Barbara busy with their new Department of Homeworld Security, this is a perfect opportunity to establish a means to funnel Earth's resources to other planets. My Lyrian kin have left their smuggling routes from Earth free for the taking."

This didn't sit well with Serac. Craig and Barbara might not be actively smuggling at the moment, but they had already laid claim to Earth. And they were fearsome opponents. Hank's connection to them only protected him, not his crew.

But Hank was the captain. Serac would follow his orders.

"I will do as you say," Serac said, bowing his head.

"One more thing."

Something else?

Serac took another deep breath to calm himself, willing his body to remain under his control.

"A personal delivery," Hank said, that same grin splitting the blue skin of his face. "I think it's time to send Craig and Barbara my little Payback."

The air chilled around Serac further. This mission would be complicated, and not just because of all the unusual parameters.

Even so, his *zlyn* urged him to agree.

Serac nodded. "Yes, sir."

Hank leaned back further in his chair and chuckled. "Prepare your ship."

Serac exited the command center quickly, eager to get this mission underway and behind him. And yet, there was something at the edge of his consciousness that made him wonder at what lay ahead. Something almost like...hope.

He grabbed the sides of the ladder, placing his feet outside the rungs and quickly sliding down several levels. As soon as his feet hit the floor, he let out a sigh that frosted the metal before him.

"Looks like I'm heading to Earth," he said.

—

The *Department of Homeworld Security* series is moving full-speed ahead, with more exciting adventures coming up in Harbor and beyond! Be sure to join my newsletter so you don't miss anything!

I love mixing up my Scifi Romance with Paranormal Romance elements. If you're a fan of that kind of mashup as well, check out my *Blades of Janus* series! These dark, long reads will have you up late at night turning the pages —and sleeping with the lights on. Here's an excerpt from the first novel, *Pack*.

Pack

The Blades of Janus
Book One

...he couldn't be a werewolf. If he was, she'd be dead already.

Tall, dark, and derpy was staring at her again. Tessa felt like she was in one of those movies where the main characters kept gazing meaningfully into each other's eyes.

In another world, she would have been absolutely down with that. Barring his strange fashion sense, this guy was just the type to get her motor revving. But this was the world she was stuck in. She couldn't afford to get sidetracked by…cosplaying hipster hotties? She hadn't quite figured him out, with his nerdy glasses, long black duster, and muscled physique.

"You have any drinks tonight?" she said.

"No."

She shook her head. "That's too bad. The first time you see something you can't explain, it really pisses off your brain. I was hoping you could rationalize it away with alcohol."

"I don't need to rationalize anything."

"Okay. The denial route is a popular choice."

Plenty of people refused to believe their senses when they saw their first dweller. After a while, they could come up with explanations for what they had "really seen". It used to be that people would tell stories about demons and monsters. Nowadays, it was usually just stress or weirdoes running around on the streets.

If they only knew the truth…

This guy was taking what he'd seen a little too calmly. He might be bottling things up, only to freak out later. Sometimes people developed a nervous tic or habit. Sometimes they lashed out at others. If that was the case, Tessa wouldn't be around long enough to do damage control. She did what she could in the moment.

"I think you might be in shock," she said.

"I'm not in shock."

"Everybody thinks that when they see a monster for the first time. But trust me, you are. Do you have someone you can call?"

"Yes."

"Good."

She didn't have to feign her smile. She was glad to be reminded that people were still helping each other out. Not everyone was alone. Part of why she was a hunter was to help preserve that life for others.

Sir Hipster Derpalot needed a plausible lie for a completely implausible situation. She looked him up and down again, and came up with just the thing.

"You can regale them with your story of getting caught up in somebody else's cosplay that was so realistic it freaked you out a little. If you tell it often enough, you'll even start to believe it."

She pulled away from him—more reluctantly than she cared to admit—then cupped his elbow, hoping to gently lead him to the entrance of the alley. He wouldn't budge.

"Look, things are about to get *really* weird here," she said. "Denial can only go so far and the human psyche is more fragile than you think. I need you elsewhere."

"I'm not leaving you alone with…"

He glanced over her shoulder at the five paralyzed

Redcaps. The five *temporarily* paralyzed Redcaps. She wasn't sure how long the battery would last on the device that was keeping them immobilized, and she had a lot of work ahead of her.

"It's okay," she said, even though it wasn't. "And who says I'm going to be alone?"

She craned her arm up behind her so she could reach one of the weapons she kept hidden beneath her jacket and pulled it out—a shortened baseball bat made of ash wood. She had sharpened the handle to a point and added electrical tape to improve the grip. It made a pretty good stake for vampires or she could go all cavewoman on things that needed squishing.

In the end, Redcaps were just giant bugs.

Giant *space* bugs.

That was the punchline to the joke that was her life. Humans told stories about scary monsters as if they all had evolved in parallel. They had no idea the monsters under the bed or lurking in the closet were aliens.

She spun the weapon like a baton, ending with the bludgeoning side at the ready. If Derpy saw that she could handle herself, maybe he'd go away.

"Not many people would keep it together as well as you're doing," she said. "I appreciate you wanting to help."

When he didn't say anything, she asked, "What's your name?"

"Marcus."

"I'm Tessa."

She switched her bat to her off hand and reached out to him in greeting. He stared at her hand for a moment before grasping it.

His skin was warm and much smoother than she'd expected. He stepped closer again.

The light was glinting off of his glasses, making it hard to see his eyes. She could tell his lashes were as dark and thick as his hair. The color of his eyes was hard to make out. A pale amber. Almost…gold.

Her skin prickled as adrenaline flowed through her system, priming her body for action. She pulled her hand back, but didn't step away.

Maybe he was wearing contacts. Maybe he was deep into playing dress-up superhero. If his mind was rationalizing what he'd seen by telling him this was all part of some game, that would explain why he was refusing to leave. After seeing a Redcap open its mouth, anybody would have trouble figuring out what was real.

He still should be freaking out a little. She didn't get how he could seem so calm.

Unless he'd encountered a monster before. Maybe something worse than Redcaps.

If Marcus had…she wasn't sure if he'd made it out human. Gold eyes—if his eyes *were* gold—only belonged to a few types of dwellers. Including one of the most dangerous.

Werewolves.

They were the result of yet another microscopic parasite that spread through the human body after it was bitten while the alien DNA was fully activated. Or, in layman's terms, when the werewolf was in its hybrid form. The parasite would infect human cells at an incredible rate, transforming their DNA into something…else.

Tessa wasn't sure if the parasites knew what they were creating or it was just random chance that they made human-alien hybrids that resembled wolves. Maybe they came from a planet of wolf-people?

It didn't matter. What concerned her was the fact that the end results were utterly deadly. Werewolves were violent killing machines whose primary prey was humans.

Marcus had said he had someone he could call. If he was a werewolf, he wouldn't need a phone. All of his packmates would be able to communicate telepathically.

But he couldn't be a werewolf. If he was, she'd be dead already. And then he'd be in for a *real* surprise.

—

About the Author

USA Today Bestselling author Cassandra Chandler uses her vivid imagination to make the world more interesting, spawning the ideas she turns into her whimsical Science Fiction romcoms and darkly evocative Paranormal and Urban Fantasy Romances. Fast-paced and funny, lighthearted or dark, her stories will introduce you to characters you want to be friends with and worlds where you'd like to build a vacation home.